"The action of saving or being saved from sin, error, or evil."

When police officer Steve Breakstone worked the toughest area in town, the only way he could survive was to imagine he was bulletproof. However, that was far from reality.

As Breakstone humbles himself and discovers a life dedicated to Jesus, he decided to help others who are in the worst of situations, like Joe, a leader of guys hustling the hood. If Breakstone could bring Joe to church, then anything was possible.

Everything seemed to change on the day Breakstone and Joe walked into God's House, with Joe speaking to the congregation and turning his life over to Jesus.

However, things turned for the worse when Joe is gunned down and killed. Breakstone is the first on the scene, asking God why He would take Joe's life when he finally turned it around.

This story will help you overcome humbling moments in your own life, strengthen your relationship with Jesus and help others do the same.

Copyright 2017 by Steve Breakstone and 9 Minute Books

All rights reserved.

No part of this publication may be reproduced, stored in a retrieval system, transmitted in any form or by any means, electronic, mechanical, photocopying, recording, or otherwise, without the written permission of the publisher and author/illustrator.

Cover Design and Book Layout by Brand Eleven Eleven, 9 Minute Books

Cover Art by Pete Mancinelli of PM Freelance

For information regarding permission or speaking engagements, contact Steve Breakstone at 941-737-0107.

REDEMPTION OF JOE

by

Steve Breakstone

Re•demp•tion

"The action of saving or being saved from sin, error, or evil."

"For He rescued us from the domain of darkness and transferred us to the kingdom of His beloved Son, in whom we have redemption (and) the forgiveness of sins." ~ Colossians 1:13-14

1

It had been a peaceful night. Steve Breakstone had actually been thinking about his kids when the radio came to life, "10-71, shots fired, 27th and Maple." The dispatcher's voice was calm, but it didn't ease Breakstone's heart which began thumping into his chest.

Breakstone flicked on his lights and stepped on the gas, imagining exactly what he would do once he arrived on the scene. He was the closest officer in the area, so he would be first to assess the situation and take control.

Breakstone went over his training as he sped down the empty streets.

Park at a safe distance and take cover.

Create a barrier between myself and the gunman.

Draw my gun.

Command that the shooter drop his weapon and lie on the ground.

Breakstone went over in his mind how he would speak to the gunman. The way he spoke could be the difference of whether or not shots would be fired in his direction, along with endangering the lives of officers who would arrive shortly after.

Keep my gun in my dominate hand, leaving my other hand free to radio in updates.

If the gunman doesn't follow Breakstone's instructions or makes a threatening movement, he would have to make a split-second decision.

As Breakstone rounded the corner, he considered it was possible that the suspect was someone he crossed paths with before. This was his area and he knew all the threats.

Despite that, which threat would it be? Who lost their temper tonight?

Breakstone arrived and hit the brakes. He noticed two bodies on the ground. He exited the car, gun drawn, scanning the area for the gunman.

It was obvious the gunman had left the scene. Breakstone updated the dispatcher and hurried to the two bodies, keeping his gun drawn while shifting his eyes in every direction.

The first body was face down. Breakstone crouched, looking at pool of blood. Suddenly the body moved, turning to the side.

It was Tibby, Joe's brother.

Breakstone quickly moved to the second body and kneeled down, breathing heavy, not wanting to believe what he was seeing.

"Joe…" Breakstone whispered, then holstered his weapon and gently placed his fingers on Joe's bloody neck, checking for a pulse.

He was dead.

2

What you are about to read is based on true events. It may seem unreal, but this actually happened.

When Steve Breakstone was in eleventh grade, he headed off to school like any normal day, approached his locker, and used his key to unlock the padlock. He reached up for his books, but noticed something towards the rear of the locker.

He paused, darting his eyes in both directions of the hallway, knowing that the note wasn't his. He didn't leave it here and there was no way for someone to get into his locker without breaking the padlock.

It's possible someone shoved the note into the upper vent of the locker, but the pure physics of the idea made it impossible.

So what was on this mysterious piece of paper? For some reason, he had an unsettling feeling.

With a trembling hand, he reached up and retrieved the note, unfolded it, then read the words which appeared to be written in blood.

Stay away from her. She can never love you like I can.

We were meant to be together.

Ashtoreth

Young Breakstone was both confused and terrified at the same time. Who would write this in blood? Who was Ashtoreth? How did they get it into his locker? What did it mean?

With the note in hand, he hurried to the one person who seemed to know a little bit about everything…

Mr. Ross, the Librarian.

Breakstone approached Mr. Ross and showed him the note. "Can you-" Before Breakstone could finish his sentence, Mr. Ross stumbled back, turned pale white, eyes, wide like saucers.

He then whispered, "That note is a curse."

Breakstone nervously smiled. "Curse? What do you mean?"

Mr. Ross didn't take his eyes off the bloody note. "Where did you get it?"

"My locker. I don't know how it got there."

There was a long, torturous moment of silence.

Mr. Ross blinked a few times and came back to reality. "The note…it's from a devil goddess."

Breakstone couldn't tell if Mr. Ross was playing a sick joke, or he was legitimately terrified. "What devil goddess?"

Mr. Ross locked his eyes on Breakstone and said with a voice that was barely audible, as if speaking the name would bring horror to all those around him. "Ashtoreth." He then pointed to the note. "Take it to the principal's office right away."

As instructed, Breakstone hurried to the principal's office and showed him the bloody note. Immediately, the principal called the police.

The note was taken from Breakstone and never mentioned again.

It would be many years later before Breakstone discovered the meaning of what the bloody note meant…

3

Breakstone was in the U.S. Army Infantry in Alaska for three years. With a knack and passion for the army, he was promoted to E4 corporal in record time, along with becoming the number one driver of the Small Unit Support Vehicle (SUSV), also known as Snow Kat.

In fact, Breakstone worked hard enough to make sure he was number one at everything he did.

During a squad live fire training, Breakstone had the fastest time and a perfect score on target hits. Later he received an award for excellent performance during the Commanding General's Marksmanship Competition on the M16 Team.

While on a mission called, "Yukon Jack," Breakstone fought through -30 degree weather conditions and received an award for his dedication.

4

When Breakstone decided to become a police officer in Sarasota, he received the highest scores in every category during his three month training. Breakstone was on the top of the world with a bulletproof feeling until one day he was called into the office and received some unsettling news.

"Steve. I'm sorry, but there's a chance we may fire you."

Breakstone couldn't believe his ears. "What? I'm getting top scores. Actually, I'm getting smokin' scores! I'm working hard and-"

The training command officer put his hand up. "There's a problem. You're not afraid of anything...including death. In fact, you're scaring us. You take everything to the extreme and I'm afraid it may cloud your judgment."

Breakstone: "Oh, well, I was just trying to do a good job."

Training Command Officer: "Here's some advice. Ask your instructors for help and learn from them instead of trying to do everything on your own. We'll see how it goes."

Breakstone agreed.

At this point, most people would have prayed to God for wisdom, faith, and courage. Breakstone believed God existed, but he didn't need God in his life, especially right now. He was bulletproof. Breakstone fought through a tough childhood, survived a divorce, made it through the army and was close to making it through police training all on his own.

God didn't help him one bit. In fact, depending on God for strength would be damaging to Breakstone and prevent him from having the courage to solve problems on his own.

As for the warning from the training officer, Breakstone agreed to take it down a notch, learn more, and show a slight weakness here and there to make them happy. He made it through training and became a Sarasota Police Officer.

5

During his first couple of weeks, Breakstone was assigned a Field Training officer. When they received their first call, Breakstone was pumped up. He didn't have butterflies, like most rookie officers. Instead, he was anxious to get started.

They arrived at a Key West style house with reports of domestic violence. Two male roommates were fighting. One had a knife and the other was attempting to grapple the knife away.

Breakstone ignored his Field Training officer who was calling for backup. He bolted into the house, knocked one guy away while snatching the knife from the other guy.

With both men in handcuffs, the Field Training officer pulled Breakstone to the side. "You should have waited for backup."

Breakstone glanced at the two men. "I didn't want them to hurt themselves."

"That's not procedure. You need to wait for backup. From this point on, I don't care if it's a routine traffic stop, you call for backup."

Breakstone didn't want to start his career off with a warning letter so he simply responded, "Yes, sir."

"Also, if you want me to pass your trial period, you'll need to do something for me over the next two weeks."

"Anything. I'm here to learn."

The Field Training officer glared at Breakstone and said with a stern voice, "Over the next two weeks, I want you to pretend you're afraid of being killed."

6

Over the years, Breakstone kept his bulletproof feeling. He didn't admit this to his superiors of course.

Eventually Breakstone was given the worst part of Sarasota. It was full of drug dealers, users, gangs, and thieves, violence in every sense of the word, rapists, and murderers.

If Breakstone didn't have the bulletproof confidence in which he worked so hard to build, one of the thugs on the street would sense his weakness and Breakstone would end up dead.

God wasn't going to save this neighborhood. Breakstone was the only line of defense.

7

Breakstone guided Joe Lawson into the cell and slammed it shut. Joe, a black man in his early twenties was built like a defensive end with tattoos covering his arms and body along with a few random scars. Both of Joe's hands and knuckles were bloody with cuts. Despite all the decorative tattoos and battle scars, Joe was actually a good looking man.

Joe turned, gripping the bars, glaring at Breakstone. "You got nothin' on me. I be back on the street before your shift is over!"

Breakstone was a bit shorter than Joe, older, built more like a drill sergeant. He stepped up to bars, locked eyes on Joe and smiled. "If you want to be back on the street, my suggestion is you start praying right now." He turned and walked away.

"I ain't prayin'!" Joe yelled from behind. "I'm the god of my life!"

Breakstone sighed and kept walking.

8

Shirley had been overweight for many years, however, it might have been because she's the best pie maker in church. There was one thing for sure, nothing was bigger than her heart or her smile.

She opened the stove, lifted her latest pie creation with an oven mitt and gently placed it on the kitchen table.

The phone rang.

Shirley grabbed her aluminum cane and wobbled to the phone and answered.

"Mom. I need bailed out."

Shirley sighed. She was going to ask what Joe did this time, but instead she responded by saying, "It will be a couple of days when my check arrives.

Sorry, honey."

"I don't have a couple of days! I need out!"

Shirley kept her voice calm. "It's the best I can do."

"Can't you borrow the money?"

A layer of sweat formed on Shirley's forehead. She glanced at her pie and said, "I'll see you in two days."

Before Joe could argue, she hung up.

9

Two days later, Shirley drove to the police station as the sun rose into the sky on another blessed morning. She sang to herself, "It is well, it is well, with my soul."

When arriving at the station, Shirley used all of her weight on the aluminum cane, moving slowly with her purse slung over her shoulder. By the time she reached the front desk, she was wheezing and out of breath.

A female officer looked up and asked, "Can I help you?"

Shirley wiped a river sweat flowing down her face and dumped her purse on the tray directly under the bulletproof clear window. A small wad of twenties fell out, along with a few coins. "I'm here…" Deep breath. "To bailout my son, Joe Lawson."

The officer spun in her chair, tapped on her computer, opened a filing cabinet and slid several forms under the tray, then waited for Shirley to take them. "You can have a seat while filling these out." The officer looked at the cash and coins. "It will be three hundred and fifty dollars."

Shirley blinked several times, pulled in another deep breath and sat down at the nearest chair, filling out the forms.

10

Joe signed his release form and was handed his personal items: keys, cellphone and a wad of cash. He pocketed all of them before stepping into the hallway where his mother had been waiting on a bench.

"I'm ready," Joe said to her. "We can go."

Shirley took a moment, pushing herself up on the aluminum cane, then walking next to her son. "I'm not going to ask what you did, because at this point, it doesn't matter. You can't keep going through life-"

"Save it, mom," Joe said, opening the door. He waited impatiently while she wobbled through.

The morning air was cool. Joe breathed it in as the scent of freedom gave him renewed strength.

Two police officers walked by, both giving Joe a glare. He smiled back at them, knowing how defenseless they were.

Speaking of defenseless, Breakstone stepped out of his cruiser and headed in their direction. He approached Shirley first, who was a few steps behind Joe. "Do you need any help?"

"No," Shirley said, wiping a layer of sweat from her face. "I need the exercise."

"I'm Officer Steve Breakstone, the one who arrested your son."

"Oh," Shirley stopped to catch her breath. "I'm Shirley."

Breakstone turned, locking eyes with Joe. "I see your mom bailed you out again."

"I told you I'd be back on the street."

"Yes you did." He looked at Shirley. "Listen, I think Joe is a smart kid, making the wrong decisions. I also think he'll have enough intelligence to change his life for the better."

Joe stomped forward, fists closed. "Don't talk about me like I'm not here!"

Shirley surprised Joe with a hard slap to the face. "When you gonna learn? I won't be here forever to bail you out!"

Joe's face softened for just a brief moment. His eyes shifted to Breakstone. "Watch your back. The police think they run things like Babylon, but I'm the ruler of the streets."

"I see." Breakstone shook Shirley's hand again. "Nice meeting you."

"And I'll pray for you," Shirley replied. "I'll be prayin' for both of you."

In a strange moment, both Joe and Breakstone stood next to each other, staring at Shirley.

11

During a drug surveillance at 8:45 p.m., Breakstone and other officers witnessed a known drug dealer named Troy Linwood Harland conduct several deals.

As the officers quickly approached, the latest buyer took off. Harland also tried to escape, however Breakstone was able to grab his arm. Harland tossed the bag of drugs at the other officers, reached down with his free hand, grabbed a broken bottle and swung it at Breakstone.

The bottle ripped into Breakstone's chin, causing hot pain to surge through his face. Despite the blood and pain, Breakstone was able to grapple Harland to the ground with the help of the other officers and place handcuffs on his wrists.

In the bag, officers found 28 packages of crack cocaine and $35 dollars (all in one dollar increments.)

Breakstone received stiches, along with a small scar.

As for Harland, he was charged, then released on bail for $10,000.

12

Joe walked up to a white male with low baggy wide-legged jeans, new white t-shirt, a thick gold chain around his neck and white K Swiss shoes.

"Yo, Duncan," Joe said, slapping hands with him and pulling him in for a quick hug. "You got the money?"

Duncan looked around. "I heard you'd been caged for last two days."

"So? I'm out." Joe inched forward, looking down at Duncan. "You got it or not?"

"Yeah, I got it. Follow me." They walked between two office buildings and stood next to a dumpster. "Where's my stuff?"

Joe handed him a set of keys. "It's the white Ford parked down the street."

Duncan looked in both directions of the alley. He reached in his pocket for a set of keys. "What did they get you for?"

Joe's face crunch with anger. "We doin' this or not?"

"Yeah…here." Duncan handed Joe the set of keys. "Blue Chrysler in the lot."

Joe gripped the keys without saying another word and headed out of the alley, turned left, walking at a fast pace to the parking lot. He then moved quickly past the cars, finding the blue Chrysler and unlocked the trunk.

Inside was a duffle bag. Joe opened it, shifted through the cash, then zipped it back up. He took a quick look around, closed the trunk, wiped the trunk with his shirt and placed the keys on the rear driver's side tire.

Joe gripped the duffle bag and took a different way back to his car so he and Duncan wouldn't cross paths. The keys were on the rear driver's side. He snatched them up, climbed into the car and plopped the duffle bag on the seat.

Feeling good about the deal, he fired up the engine and sped off.

13

While on patrol, Breakstone received a call that a woman was holding a steak knife and the boyfriend was attempting to get it away from her. It wasn't clear if the woman was trying to stab the boyfriend, or attempt suicide.

Breakstone pulled into the driveway and quickly arrived at the front door. He pushed it open and looked inside to get an understanding of the situation. Two people were shouting at each other in the living room area.

Suddenly a German Shepard appeared and lunged forward at Breakstone. He backed up, made his way to the yard, keeping his eyes on the dog.

The German Shepard once again lunged forward and Breakstone was able to sidestep out of the way. He drew his weapon, aimed, and waited to see if the dog would back off.

It didn't.

Instead, the Shepard jumped at Breakstone. He squeezed the trigger, hitting the dog in the mouth.

The boyfriend inside the house came running out. Behind him was the woman who tossed the steak knife to the side and hurried to the dog, hugging it and crying.

Breakstone called for help on his shoulder radio. The boyfriend drove the dog to the veterinarian as Breakstone followed.

When the media got a hold of the story, the article stated that the girl was attempting to commit suicide and the boyfriend called 911 for help as he fought to get the knife away from her.

The article discussed Breakstone shooting the German Shepard. Also, when the boyfriend returned from the veterinarian, he discovered his girlfriend on the floor, covered in the dog's blood, crying hysterically. Officers never questioned the girl to see if she was suicidal and if she needed medical treatment. Instead, they just left her there alone.

The boyfriend made a statement in the article, "They shot our dog and they just left my girlfriend in the house without getting her any sort of treatment for her thoughts of suicide. The police actually made matters worse!"

The journalist finished the article by saying, "Maybe 911 isn't always the best call to make."

This was Breakstone's first bad press. Although he was perfectly correct to shoot the dog and was cleared of any charges, it didn't look good how things turned out, especially since this was apparently a suicide call, not a knife fight between two lovers.

Breakstone knew he wasn't perfect and was happy to learn the dog made a full recovery. However, this was one of many learning experiences as a police officer, and the first of many dealings with the media.

14

One early morning in the briefing room during shift change, information was given to Breakstone about a suspect, John L. Bean, who was on a three day crime rampage. It was noted that Ben could be armed with a .357 Magnum that he stole from a security guard.

Just as Breakstone got a cup of coffee and left the briefing room, he received a call that Officer Eddie Howell may have spotted Bean.

Breakstone hurried to his cruiser and a few minutes later, tracked down Bean in a stolen maroon Cadillac and chased him for several miles until Bean crashed into a hotel.

Breakstone then hurried on foot with his weapon drawn. He looked inside the Cadillac.

Bean was gone.

Breakstone's eyes darted in every direction. He saw Bean racing towards a residential area. Breakstone updated the dispatcher while chasing. "Stop! Police!"

Bean didn't stop. In fact, Breakstone had an image of Bean turning around and firing his gun to get away.

As sirens approached, Breakstone closed the gap on Bean. "Stop!" Breakstone yelled again.

Bean was clearly running out of steam. He turned towards a house, broke down the door and entered.

Breakstone was just seconds behind. He had one chance to enter the home and find Bean, or there would be a hostage situation.

Three people had appeared from the bedroom. Obviously they had been sleeping. "Stay there!" Breakstone yelled.

He walked through the home, keeping his weapon in front. Bean was in the kitchen, trapped.

"It's over," Breakstone said.

Bean raised his gun and was about to fire. Breakstone quickly squeezed the trigger five times. The first shot hit Bean in the wrist.

Second shot grazed Bean's lower leg.

Despite being shot twice, Bean continued pointing the gun.

Breakstone fired three more quick shots. He hit the wall, a book and the fridge. Those of course were warning shots, because Breakstone could have easily killed the man.

Bean tossed the gun down and surrendered.

15

Breakstone dressed in a t-shirt and jeans, sitting in a junk car used for undercover. He parked on the corner of Leon and Osprey at 10:00 p.m.

The biggest drug dealer in town nicknamed Ebab, was tall, imposing and built like a mountain. Next to him was his right hand man nicknamed Cadillac, a thinner version of Ebab with corn rows, gold teeth and two long scars over his right eye.

Breakstone would never admit this to anyone, but it broke his heart seeing the regular stream of teenagers and adults approaching Cadillac to buy drugs while Ebab stood off in the distance, watching over the business. If the police raided the corner, Cadillac would be caught, but Ebab would slip into the shadows and escape.

This was a never ending battle that Breakstone vowed to remove, but at this point he was barely disrupting the drug business in town.

After about an hour, something caught the attention of Breakstone. A boy about eleven-years-old wearing a Raiders jersey approached Ebab, handing him a paper bag. Breakstone leaned forward over the steering wheel, suddenly recognizing the boy. His name is Tonker, a kid from the streets and a talented football player.

Tonker disappeared into the shadows as a thin woman approached Ebab. He reached into the bag and exchanged drugs for money as she passed by. It was much smoother and more discreet than what Cadillac was doing on the opposite corner.

Tonker once again appeared from the shadows and replaced the empty paper bag with another one, then hurried off.

Breakstone sighed, opened the door and headed around the corner so Ebab and Cadillac couldn't see him.

Breakstone slipped between two houses and watched Tonker reach into the passenger seat of a black Chevy, grab a paper bag and hurry off. Breakstone followed Tonker and grabbed him just before he arrived back to Ebab.

Tonker attempted to throw the paper bag, but Breakstone quickly snatched it from his hand and looked inside.

It was filled with vials of crack.

Breakstone shouted to Ebab and Cadillac, "Don't either of you move!"

Surprisingly, they actually approached Breakstone while the people who had arrived to buy drugs scurried like roaches.

Breakstone let go of Tonker's jersey. "Is your brother Deoley in the Chevy back there?"

"Yes, sir," Tonker said in a soft voice.

Breakstone tipped over the paper bag, letting the vials of crack drop to the sidewalk. He then stepped on them, crushing each one with his boot. "You boys are done for the night."

Cadillac smiled, showing his gold teeth. "You're ballsy for a dead man."

Breakstone knew that both Cadillac and Ebab were carrying guns. In fact, they probably had more than one gun on them.

Breakstone looked at Tonker. "You're about a ten minute walk from home. I suggest you use that speed of yours and get there in five."

Tonker didn't hesitate. He spun on his heels and ran in a full sprint down the sidewalk.

Breakstone looked at Cadillac, then shifted his eyes to Ebab. "This corner is closed for business."

Cadillac cocked his head. "I say different."

Ebab put his hand up. "Nope. It's cool."

Breakstone knew Ebab was a smart businessman. Attacking a police officer, even verbally would shut their business down for months, rather than a few hours. This was just a pinprick having to leave the corner tonight.

16

Joe had been watching everything from down the street. Next to him was his brother Tibby. Both were quite, waiting to see if Cadillac was actually going to pull his gun and shoot Breakstone.

It didn't happen.

Joe reached in his pocket and handed Tibby a wad of cash. "Take this and stay away from the corner."

Tibby shoved the cash in his jeans and walked away.

After Breakstone drove off, Joe stood under the street light so Ebab and Cadillac could see him.

Deoley pulled up to the corner in the black Chevy, picked up Ebab and Cadillac, then drove them to Joe. All three climbed out of the car.

Joe locked eyes on each of them. "Did Breakstone get the cash?"

Ebab: "No. Just shut us down for the night." He handed Joe a wad wrapped in a rubber band. "You always win, Joe. Could be drugs, cards, dice…doesn't matter. You always win."

Deoley: "The problem is, we do all the risk. Joe just in the background collecting money."

Joe lifted the wad of cash. "You want my money, Deoley? It's here." He slipped it into his pocket while looking at Deoley with a grin. "Come get it."

Without warning, Joe closed his fist and connected on Ebab's jaw, then threw another punch at Cadillac, busting open his cheek. Joe quickly moved to Deoley, standing face-to-face. He reached in Deoley's shirt, pulled the gun out and shoved it in Deoley's hand.

"Men use their fists," Joe said. "Boys need guns."

Ebab and Cadillac regained their senses, standing like nothing happened. Deoley shoved the gun back in his belt and said, "Breakstone."

Joe: "What about him?"

Deoley: "He must have juice on you. It's why he keeps comin'."

Joe surprised Deoley with a punch square on his nose. A fountain of blood poured down his face. "I run the street. Not you. Not Ebab, Cadillac and not some broken down cowboy named Breakstone. You got me?"

Joe walked away, giving Deoley and the others a chance to pull their guns and shoot him in the back.

Nothing happened.

He was bulletproof.

17

Joe made it home the next morning. He walked inside the house, passing the picture of Jesus on the wall, following the smell of breakfast in the kitchen. Joe kissed his mom on the cheek as she flipped bacon on the stove. "Mornin', mama."

Shirley barely acknowledged him. "I suppose you hungry."

Joe slid off his jacket. "Starvin'."

Shirley finished making breakfast and slid a plate in front of Joe. As he grabbed a fork, Shirley placed her hand on his and prayed.

18

The hours Breakstone kept became sporadic, not to mention working days off to reduce crime. Breakstone and his taskforce team in three months made 129 felony arrests, 219 misdemeanor arrests, wrote 327 traffic citations, 55 bicycle citations, served 49 warrants, 31 prostitution arrests, and made 68 drug related arrests.

In addition, the unit conducted 5 prostitution stings, 2 clean sweep operations, 3 theft decoy details, 3 traffic operations, and 12 narcotics search warrants while busting drug operations.

This was all in one neighborhood.

Joe's neighborhood.

Over the next nine months, Breakstone personally seized 218 cocaine rocks and 37 baggies of marijuana. Street corners were no longer an easy place for dealers to sell drugs.

Breakstone also joined a task force that took down a drug ring, confiscating over 250 grams of marijuana and $1,676.00 in drug money.

He found drugs hidden in soda cans and bags, stashed behind trees. On foot, he would walk along known drug areas and find their hiding spots.

From there, Breakstone began teaching other officers how to locate hidden drugs, along with the "tricks of the trade" conducted by dealers.

The streets and sidewalks weren't made for drug dealers. Neighborhood sidewalks were made for kids to ride their bikes, for people to walk, and children to arrive home safely from school.

Until every drug was found and every dealer was in jail, Breakstone made his personal mission to walk down every sidewalk and let people like Joe understand that business was closed.

19

Breakstone and his wife Angela walked out of the marriage counselor's office. He kissed her on the cheek, unable to look her directly in the eyes. "I'm going to keep trying. I'll do it for you and the kids."

A tear slid from Angela's eye. "You keep saying that."

After being married nine years they were basically roommates. They never fought or got in argument. They didn't have parenting skills or have experience on how a husband and wife should act.

Breakstone raced motorcycles to blow off steam. When he felt a lot of pressure, he would meet the guys from the police department at the bar and suck down pitchers of beer. Most of the time, they would close the place down.

Angela never complained. She had her own friends and made her own plans.

There wasn't the bond of love to keep Breakstone and Angela together and certainly not a bond with Christ to show them how a husband and wife with a child should love each other.

Breakstone decided to attend church. There wasn't a specific reason, other than it seemed like the right thing to do. Even Angela joined him, although, it was like two friends attending a service.

During that time a friend of his, John Malone, got a group of guys together and approached Breakstone. Malone said, "Steve, we've been praying for you."

Breakstone forced a grin. How could he respond? He simply said, "Um…okay."

Week after week, month after month, year after year, this went on. "Steve, we've been praying for you."

Breakstone didn't understand. He went to church. What else did they want from him? Why did they single him out and continue offering their prayers? Weren't there other people who needed God's help more than him?

Despite Breakstone having marriage problems, along with pressures as a police officer, there wasn't a need for a group of men to add him to their prayers. He could handle things just fine.

After all, Breakstone was bulletproof.

He wanted to tell the group of men, "Pray for someone who actually needs it!"

Breakstone was living up to his last name…he wouldn't break.

John, leader of the men's group finally said, "Maybe we're praying for the wrong man? God hasn't made a dent in your life."

Actually, Breakstone had been using God to move forward, but more as a symbol. He really didn't need God's love, wisdom, or power. A little bit of church here and there made his life complete.

God was for the weaker guys.

If Breakstone relied on God, it would deteriorate him and could cost his life on the job. Breakstone had to remain tough on the street with a neighborhood full of gangs, drugs, and shootings.

Yes…God was for the weak.

20

It was early in the night when Breakstone was assigned to the Street Level Tactical Unit. Instead of his uniform, he wore jeans and a windbreaker over his vest.

Breakstone drove to the Kingsway Apartments, parked his unmarked vehicle and walked down the sidewalk. He noticed Deoley had a backpack over one arm, dealing right in front of the apartments in plain sight.

Breakstone shook his head and said to himself, "You're getting sloppy, Deoley."

Actually, it was more likely that Deoley, along with Joe, Ebab, Cadillac, and all the other thugs in town were feeling above the law and untouchable.

Well, it was going to end tonight.

Breakstone used his radio, called it in, and continued forward.

Deoley saw Breakstone, turned and sprinted into the front doorway of the Kingsway apartments. Breakstone chased after him, using his shoulder radio to update the dispatcher.

He chased Deoley up the stairs filled with a mixture of toys and empty beer bottles. They sprinted down the hallway to the other side, back down the stairs and exited the rear of the building.

Deoley tossed his backpack over the fence and kept running. Breakstone felt the air slip away from his lungs, but he kept going, not wanting to let Deoley get away.

They reached a large chain link fence. Deoley scurried up in quick fashion. Breakstone climbed, but his shoulder radio got caught on his windbreaker, then snagged between a link on the fence, tugging him back and ripping the jacket.

Breakstone kept climbing while attempting to tear his shoulder radio free from the fence.

On the other side he leaped down, took a few steps, then was surprised by Deoley sprinting at him.

Deoley collided so hard against Breakstone into the fence, he felt the wind from his lungs blow out his mouth. The shoulder radio fell to the ground like a broken Slinky as Deoley attempted to grab Breakstone's pistol. Breakstone used one hand to clutch Deoley's neck while using the other hand to press down on Deoley's wrist.

Deoley's face was so close, his sweat drizzled down Breakstone's cheek. Deoley had a firm grip on the pistol and must have sensed Breakstone losing his strength.

Deoley then smiled. "Just give up." It was creepy, as if spoken by Satan himself. Deoley then whispered, "Let the thoughts of your family slip from your mind. You're done. Give up…"

This enraged Breakstone. He summoned all his strength and said, "I don't know what give up means."

Breakstone continued holding Deoley's wrist down, not letting him pull the pistol up from the holster while using his other hand to squeeze Deoley's neck.

Sirens could be heard in the distance.

Breakstone had to make a decision, because he couldn't hold off Deoley much longer. He let go of Deoley's wrist and quickly punched him in the ribs. He used his other hand to crush Deoley's neck.

In quick fashion, Breakstone was able to turn Deoley around and force him to the dirt. He placed a firm knee on his back and pulled Deoley's wrists behind him, squeezing on the handcuffs.

After taking a second to catch his breath, Breakstone used his cellphone to call 911. "This is Sergeant Breakstone…I…" He had to take in another deep breath. "I lost my walkie. Need assistance."

Dispatcher: "Who are you? Say again."

Breakstone formed a sarcastic grin, feeling a mix of irritation and exhaustion. "Sergeant Breakstone!" He then gave his location.

A few minutes later, two police officers raced towards him.

21

When Breakstone arrived home at two in the morning, Angela was awake, sitting on the couch. Breakstone approached her, seeing a large envelope next to her on the couch.

He pointed, asking, "What's that?"

She lifted the envelope and handed it to him. "I'm done. Inside are the details. I get full custody of the kids. There's also details in there about the affairs you've been having. It should be a nice reflection of your life."

Breakstone gripped the envelope, still feeling the pain from his battle with Deoley and now struggling to understand what was happening with Angela.

"Wait…maybe we need to see the counselor again."

Angela stood. "No more counseling. No more lies. No more failed attempts at saving this marriage. There's a house for rent, three doors down from here. I'll be packed and gone by tomorrow."

Breakstone searched for something to say, but all he could do was stand in the living room, silent, knowing he brought all this on himself.

22

Breakstone had been on lunch break at a motorcycle drag racing store, when he heard over his shoulder radio that the bank on Fruitville had been robbed. He smiled at the owner of the store and said with a bit of sarcasm, "I have to go catch a bank robber now."

While in his cruiser, Breakstone noticed a brown two-door Toyota with a white male driving. The suspect in the bank was also white, but the description of the vehicle was a gray four-door Toyota. Despite this, the robbery just happened a few minutes ago down the street. Breakstone figured he'd better at least follow the Toyota.

At the next stoplight, he noticed the driver look into the mirror, then toss a white t-shirt on the passenger seat.

Breakstone was curious. What was the guy covering up with the shirt?

Breakstone remained close behind. The driver was doing about ten miles under the speed limit. Breakstone decided to pull up to the side of the Toyota at the next light. He looked at the driver, but the guy kept his eyes forward, both hands on the steering wheel.

This was enough for Breakstone. He quickly pulled over and approached the driver on foot with one hand on his holster. He questioned him for a minute then looked on the passenger's seat. The white t-shirt had slipped off, exposing a FedEx envelope with cash sticking out, along with a photo processing envelope with bills showing. Also there was a pair of sunglasses and a pack of Marlboro's.

Then he noticed a .22 caliber handgun on the floor.

Breakstone pulled his weapon and shouted, "Don't move!"

Breakstone reached up for his shoulder radio and said, "I got the bank robber. He has a thing full of money. This is going to be our guy."

The sidewalk was clear of people, so Breakstone guided the driver out of the car to place the handcuffs on him.

Suddenly, the suspect turned and locked his eyes on Breakstone's weapon. Breakstone yelled, "Don't even think-"

The man lunged for the gun. Breakstone was able to yank it away, holster it, then grab the guy and flip him over on the sidewalk, dropping him like a bag of mulch. He kneeled down on the suspect's back and squeezed on the handcuffs.

Breathing heavy, Breakstone reached for his radio to notify the dispatcher, "Everything is ten-four."

A United Van Lines truck appeared around the corner and slowed to a stop. The driver poked his head out and yelled, "Y'all need a hand?"

Breakstone was still trying to catch his breath. "Yes. Come here and sit on this guy. He robbed a bank."

The driver quickly exited his truck, sat on the suspect, then grabbed his cellphone and made a call. "Y'all ain't going to believe this, honey! I'm sitting on a bank robber!"

Breakstone chuckled and questioned the suspect while the truck driver continued sitting on the man, making calls to his wife and friends.

Meanwhile, the suspect admitted to Breakstone that he robbed the bank, along with one other bank job.

A few weeks later, Breakstone read the FBI file on the bank robbery case. When questioned about lunging for the gun, the man replied, "Suicide by cop. I was going to kill him, or he was going to kill me."

The media never reported the struggled. Instead, the article claimed the man surrendered without resistance.

The redneck who helped Breakstone was given an award, which also wasn't reported in the newspaper.

When a reporter asked Breakstone how he was able to catch the robber, all he said were two words, "Got lucky."

23

Over the years, Breakstone became the number one ranked officer for arrests; also he achieved this faster than anyone else in the history of the department.

A drug dealer named Achilles had also been rising in the ranks, along with a brother and sister team; Tim and Myra Rainey. They paid a hitman out of Miami, Norman John, nicknamed Indian, $40,000 to kill Breakstone.

Norman arrived a few days later and waited for Breakstone at one of his regular stops in the area, which was the bar called Town Hall, located on Martin Luther King Drive.

While standing there, a black man named Michael Monkey Morris stumbled out of the bar, drunk, noticing Norman.

Morris wiped his mouth and said, "Yo…" He burped. "Go find somewhere else to stand." This turned into a shouting match.

Norman lost his temper. He reached into his pocket, pulled his gun and shot Morris three times, then took off.

24

Breakstone and several officers arrived at the Town Hall bar, seeing Michael Monkey Morris dead with three bullets in his chest. Witnesses inside the bar claimed they heard him shouting with someone.

A day later, Breakstone was told by several people on the streets there was a hit put out on him by Achilles, Tim, and Myra.

Breakstone quickly drove to the Rainey house, seeing them on the porch. Most likely they had weapons nearby.

Breakstone took off his gun holster and marched to the porch.

"I don't have a weapon on me. You both can be the heroes of Sarasota. Take your shot. Don't send someone to do your dirty work. Shoot me yourselves!" He glared at him. "I'm waiting."

Tim and Myra Rainey glanced at each other.

Breakstone narrowed his eyes. "That's what I thought. Don't ever cross the line again. I catch bad guys, this is what I do. You deal drugs. That's what you and Achilles do. Let's keep that clear without blurring the line, especially using a hot-tempered hitman."

Breakstone turned on his heels and left.

To protect his family, Breakstone gave his wife a gun. She was living three doors down and he didn't want someone walking in and killing her, along with their children.

He was honest with Angela about the hitman so that she would take it seriously. She accepted the gun and kept it in her bedroom dresser.

Also, Breakstone taught his son, Gabe, how to shoot.

A month later Norman John, the hitman who was hired to kill Breakstone, was found dead in Georgia after being shot in the face with a 12-gauge shotgun.

25

Outside of Tookie's Barber Shop, Breakstone pulled up and parked the car, feeling like his body had been used for a punching bag. He hadn't slept in days and should be home trying to rest before his shift tonight, but there was something he had to do first.

Joe had walked up, locking eyes with Breakstone. "What's it with you? I can't get my haircut now?"

Breakstone raised his hand. "Calm down. I'm here unofficially. Let's talk about Deoley."

Joe: "What about him?"

Breakstone: "He got let out of jail."

Joe: "I know."

Breakstone: "I heard on the street he's into something big."

Joe hesitated. "Nottin' to do with me."

Breakstone: "I hope not." He paused, looking around. "There's different kinds of tough. Physical toughness, which everyone pretends to have in the street." He looked at Joe. "And then there's spiritual toughness, which is stronger than anything."

Joe laughed. "What's wrong with you?"

Breakstone returned a grin. "We both have something in common. We want to be the toughest in the street, but that won't work. It's only a matter of time before the Deoley's of the world get the best of us. I say we turn our strength into something spiritual."

Joe: "Spiritual? There's notin' spiritual in the street gonna save us. Did that hitman shake you up?"

Breakstone: "More like a wakeup call. I'm certain there's only one thing that can save us both."

Joe: "You goin' soft on me, Stone?"

Breakstone thought about what to say next. He wasn't some saint. It's true that he was trying to rid the streets of crime, but were the sins he committed any better? Also, why was he talking to Joe? What led him here in the first place? He wasn't even sure. Everything was just a haze of events that brought him to the entrance of this barber shop.

Breakstone: "What about church?"

Joe: "What about it?"

Breakstone: "I'm sure your ma has tried to get you to go."

Joe: "Church don't work for me. It works for mamma."

Breakstone: "Yeah, church didn't work for me either, but I'm starting to think I was wrong." He leveled his eyes on Joe. "We both need God's help."

Joe laughed again. "I'm gonna get my haircut."

Breakstone: "I'll pick you up Sunday morning and take you."

Joe: "Sunday mornin' I get my beauty rest. Better not disrupt that."

Breakstone: "Tough guys don't back down from a challenge. You saying the men at church are stronger than you?"

Joe stared at Breakstone for a long moment, then entered the barber shop without saying another word.

Breakstone walked away, feeling even more sore and exhausted.

26

An anonymous call came in about a white and green vehicle with drugs inside. Officer Pearson located the car, but no drugs were inside and the driver was nowhere to be found.

That same night, another anonymous call came in about the green and white vehicle having weapons inside. After the officer once again located the car and searched it, no weapons were inside. Also, like before, the driver wasn't in the area.

Six days later, Breakstone rode with Pearson in the cruiser.

Pearson: "There's that green and white car someone keeps calling about. I didn't find anything, including the driver."

Breakstone watched as the car stopped at a light on 10th and Central. There were two people in the front seat. "Let's check it out."

Pearson lit up his lights and pulled the vehicle over.

The driver, Vincent Gordon age eighteen, gave Pearson permission to search the car while Breakstone kept his eye on the driver and the passenger.

Pearson found two black ski masks in the trunk. He showed Breakstone and they arrested both passengers.

During questioning at the police station, Gordon, along with the passenger and two others were charged after being linked to a series of armed robberies. During those robberies, shots had been fired at the victims and one person was murdered. These crimes had gone unsolved and the case went cold, that is, until Officer Pearson and Officer Breakstone pulled the car over during a routine traffic stop.

Both Pearson and Breakstone were commended for their actions.

27

Breakstone started a new habit of keeping a bible in his police cruiser. Every chance he read random passages. It certainly gave him some guidance and sparked a fire in his soul, but he couldn't sense the presence of God like it's discussed in the bible. He wanted to know for sure God was around, just like he was reading.

For the first time, Breakstone felt a bit of weakness. He originally blamed it on exhaustion, both physically and spiritually. Between his upcoming divorce, a hitman, drug dealers, and the daily job of trying to survive, it was wearing him down.

"You will seek Me and find Me when you search for Me with all your heart." ~ Jeremiah 29:13

28

On Sunday morning, Breakstone pulled up to Shirley and Joe's house, parking in the driveway. Was he really going to take a drug dealer into church? For that matter, was a cheating husband who was about to get a divorce the right person to bring Joe to God's House?

They would probably both burst into flames the second they stepped inside.

Breakstone sighed, then stepped out of the car, approached the front door and rang the bell.

Shirley answered, leaning on her aluminum cane.

Breakstone smiled. "Hey there, Ms. Shirley. I'm here to pick up Joe."

Shirley scrunched her eyes. "Who are you?"

"Steve Breakstone of the Sarasota Police Department. We've met before."

Shirley's face brightened. "Oh yeah! Mr. Breakstone!" She re-gripped her cane. "You here for Joe? What he done now?"

Breakstone: "Believe it or not, I'm hoping he'll come to church with me."

Tears flooded Shirley's eyes. "I've been prayin' for this day! I've been prayin' for someone to bring Joe to the light!"

Breakstone: "Well, I'm not sure if he'll even go, but here I am."

Shirley stepped to the side. "Come on in."

Before Breakstone took a step forward, Joe appeared, dressed in a tan button down shirt and black slacks. He kissed his mom on the cheek and brushed by Breakstone saying, "You comin'?"

29

Whatever happened to bring Breakstone closer to God, must have also happened to Joe. There wasn't any other explanation. Breakstone and Joe were both men who didn't need God, but somehow, decided to at least explore the idea.

It seemed like yesterday when Breakstone was shoving Joe into a cell. How could things have changed this quickly? Breakstone certainly didn't have the strength to turn some kid from the streets into faithful follower of Jesus.

In fact, Breakstone didn't have the strength to change his own bad habits, much less someone else's.

Yet, there they were, walking through the parking lot, entering the House of God.

Joe leaned close to Breakstone and whispered, "Everyone is smilin' at me. What's wrong with them?"

Breakstone whispered back, "They are just being polite. You've never experienced this before."

They shook a dozen hands before finding their seats.

Joe looked around and shifted uncomfortably in the pew. "I don't feel right."

Breakstone kept his voice low. "I don't feel much better, but let's both man-up and deal with it."

As the service began, Breakstone wondered what was going through Joe's head. He most certainly felt like an outsider. Heck, Breakstone felt the same way. The people around them were Christians. They were full of love and faith. They sang songs with joyful tears in their eyes, prayed with earnest compassion and listened to the pastor's every word, careful not to miss a single portion of his message.

Breakstone thought about how just a few streets away from the church was a neighborhood of gangs, drugs, and violence…Joe's world, along with Breakstone's assigned area.

The wall between church and crime was paper thin.

30

Breakstone had once told Joe he belonged in jail. That was probably true, but Joe belonged in this church even more than rotting in a cell.

Also Breakstone belonged in the pew, sitting next to Joe.

Breakstone had challenged Joe to come to church, but now it seemed that Breakstone was also challenging himself. He began reading the Word, but that wasn't enough. He went to church here and there, but that wasn't even close to what God wanted in Breakstone's life.

Being strong and going through the motions wasn't doing God's best. In act, it was the opposite. Breakstone needed to be humbled, on his knees and begging for God to show him glory.

Joe wouldn't last two days on the street if he backed down. It would be a sign of weakness and the wolves would attack.

If Breakstone backed down as a police officer, or backed down as a husband, father, or just being a man, it would show weakness. However, Breakstone realized now he was weak because he didn't have the courage to back down.

Joe was weak, because he couldn't walk away. He was worried about what others thought about him, just like Breakstone worried about the opinion of others.

The only opinion that mattered was God's. Breakstone now realized that more than ever.

During the sermon, Breakstone avoided looking at Joe. For some reason he didn't want to spook him, like making a sudden movement towards a squirrel and watch it scurrying away. The important thing was Joe was still in his seat, next to Breakstone, listening to the pastor wrap up his message.

Then another fear crossed Breakstone's mind. What do others think about him cheating on Angela and her filing for divorce? Were people whispering to each other when he walked inside? Surely Angela told her friends, who then told their friends, causing the gossip to spread like a brushfire.

Also, what did the congregation think about Joe? He may have been dressed in decent clothes, but he couldn't hide the years of being on the streets, fighting for every nickel and trying to survive.

Maybe Breakstone's expression exposed his own shame? Could he hide his sins in this place amongst these loving, caring people? Or could they see right through him?

Suddenly, right in the middle of the service, Joe stood up and began speaking to the minister…

31

Breakstone had been to church on and off throughout his life. He knew that no one should stand up while the pastor was preaching and have a conversation. The moment Joe stood, Breakstone felt his heart hammer against his chest.

The awkward silence seemed to last forever. Some people were appalled that Joe stood, leaning his hands on the pew, staring at the pastor. Others had a panic look on their face. Yet others were actually giggling.

Breakstone eyed two ushers who seemed ready to escort Joe out of the church. If that happened, there was no way Joe would ever return.

Finally, Joe spoke in a loud, clear voice. "I got somethin' I like to say, Reverend, if it be alright with you."

The pastor looked at the two ushers and placed his hand up, as if letting them know everything was okay. He then looked at Joe. "Yes it's okay, my friend. All are welcome to testify here."

Breakstone didn't move, yet inside, his heart banged against his chest.

Joe cleared this throat. "Well then. You see, I'm not like you all. But I'm here. I been listening to lots of you folks stand up and thank God for a whole lot of things and I guess I should thank Him too."

The entire church became silent. You could hear the wind outside, gently seeping against the building.

Pastor: "Inside this church, we say what's in our hearts. Please continue."

Joe glanced down at Breakstone, then addressed the entire congregation. "My name is Joe Lawson. I grew up here in Sarasota, like a lot of you. But I grew up on the streets. It ain't easy on the streets. I live hard and I done some hard things."

Joe looked down at Breakstone. Joe's eyes softened as the hatred inside began to seep away. He once again addressed the congregation. "Breakstone here knows me. He knows the hard things I done. He even jailed me a bunch of times. The last time he arrested me, he said jail was where I belonged. Maybe he was right."

Joe hesitated, gripping the pew in front of him. "Breakstone brought me here to this church. He didn't ask me. Instead, he challenged me to come here. He knew me well enough to know that if he challenged me, man to man, that I couldn't back down from it. You see, on the street, if you back down once, you gonna back down again. Pretty soon, you doin' nothin' but backin' down."

Joe stood tall. "You don't last long on the street if you backin' down all the time. Breakstone knows. He challenged me lots of times, but I never once backed down. Not from him, not from the police, not from gangs, not from anybody.

"But I'm here. Listenin' to you all talk. I'm listenin' to the reverend up there talkin'. I'm kinda of feelin' why all of you come back here every Sunday. I can't really put it into words…"

Joe briefly lowered his head. "I feel…love, goodness…and I guess…I want to thank you all for that feeling I now have inside of me. Here in your church, a thug from the streets, a guy you try to avoid and hope I never get to you in the dark, I'm suddenly feelin' love from you all."

Joe once again glanced at Breakstone. "But this man, Breakstone, knowing what I am, brought me here. So I got to ask myself. If Breakstone can bring me in this church and you all can make me feel this love I have right now, what else can God make me feel when I'm not here, now that I know this feelin'? What else can I do with my life?"

Joe sat back down and lowered his head, seeming lost in his own thoughts.

The pastor began clapping. The two ushers clapped. Breakstone stood up and applauded, followed by the entire congregation.

When the service ended, Breakstone and Joe headed to the car and pulled away. Breakstone remained quiet, not wanting to ruin the moment.

Instead, he let Joe have an open conversation with God.

32

During the last part of the ride home, Joe still hadn't said a word. Breakstone glanced over several times, seeing Joe gazing out the window.

As they pulled down the street, Breakstone broke the silence. "I'm sure your mom will be proud and a little emotional, but don't hold that against her."

Joe didn't respond. He just kept gazing out the window.

Breakstone pulled into the driveway and watched as Joe climbed out of the car.

Joe then leaned down, gave Breakstone a slight grin and said, "So, you'll pick me up next week?"

Breakstone had to fight back the tears. "Yeah, I'll pick you up next Sunday. Same time."

"Then Jesus spoke to them again, saying, 'I am the light of the world. He who follows Me shall not walk in darkness, but have the light of life.'" ~ John 8:12

33

Breakstone's boss called him in for a meeting.

"I heard about you taking Joe Lawson to church."

Breakstone: "Yeah I did. Why, do you want to go with us next Sunday?"

"This isn't a joke."

Breakstone: "I agree. It's not."

"You can't have familiarity with felons."

Breakstone: "I took a tough kid from the streets to church. How is that a crime?"

"Did you know Joe Lawson is under investigation for the murder at Club Mary?"

Breakstone: "He didn't do that."

"Really? How do you know?"

Breakstone: "It's not something Joe would do. I know it in my heart."

"So you're saying Joe wouldn't commit murder, but he does sell drugs, steal, and has gang affiliations, which is okay."

Breakstone: "You know I'm not saying that. I'm just saying he wasn't the one who committed the murder at Club Mary."

"There was more than one suspect, all wearing masks. Joe is a ring leader."

Breakstone: "Yes, he's the ring leader in his neighborhood. He's also a business man. A senseless murder in a strip club isn't what Joe would call, 'good business.'"

"You make him sound like a saint."

Breakstone: "He's far from that, which is why he needed church. I'm also far from being a saint, which is why I need church."

"Do you know how it looks when you arrest Joe, then take him to church?"

Breakstone: "Yes, it looks like I'm trying to bring a young man to know Jesus."

"You're not understanding what I'm trying to say. What if you saw me bust a prostitute on Friday, then you saw us in church together on Sunday? How does that look?"

Breakstone: "Honestly, like you're trying to save her soul."

"No, it's not how it would look. People would think her and I have a relationship."

Breakstone: "Are you saying that it's okay for someone to bring Joe or a prostitute to church, but it's not okay for a police officer to bring them to church?"

"Yes, it's exactly what I'm saying."

Breakstone: "Could a police dispatcher bring someone like Joe to church?"

"Well, no."

Breakstone: "Could a spouse of a police officer bring someone like Joe to church?"

"No, that wouldn't look good. It's all about how people perceive us as police officers. We need to earn the public's trust. Also, it's a slippery slope bringing men like Joe into your life."

Breakstone: "What does that mean?"

"What if Joe decides to use this opportunity to come over your house and steal your big screen. What would you do?"

Breakstone: "Arrest him."

"Then what?"

Breakstone: "Take him to church when he gets out."

"You see; that's wrong. You can't associate yourself with criminals. Maybe the next time you see Joe on the streets dealing drugs, you'll let it slide, because you don't want the church to find out he's back to his old ways."

Breakstone: "I wouldn't let a criminal slide."

"I believe you, but some journalist might not. It's all about perception."

Breakstone: "Well, here's a little bit of my perception. I believe if Joe wasn't led down this path, he would have made a terrific police officer."

"What! How could you even suggest such a thing?"

Breakstone: "Joe knows how to manage people. Believe it or not, he knows that how to solve problems. Joe runs a profitable business by connecting with people on his street. Every day he wakes up, goes to work, and knows he could be killed by some punk trying to make a name for himself. Despite that, he keeps getting up each day and walks the street."

"You're glorifying him like being a street thug is something every kid should try."

Breakstone: "No, I'm saying if Joe went down a different path, he has all the qualities of a good cop. That's it."

"But Joe didn't choose the good path; he chose this life and he'll be punished because of his choices. For that matter, if you keep up this relationship with Joe then you'll suffer the consequences as well."

Breakstone: "Listen, if you want to join Joe and I next Sunday, let me know. Otherwise, I have to get back to work."

34

When you leave the walls of church, it seems that God's protection isn't as strong. That's how Joe felt the following Monday morning as he walked his normal route to "work."

He turned the corner and saw three familiar young black men surrounding an older white man who was carrying groceries home from the store. One of the men asked for the guy's wallet while the others looked inside his groceries.

For some reason Joe lost it. On any other day, he would have just kept walking by, but today, this didn't seem right.

Joe hurried to the group and shoved the three black men, then turned to the older man and said, "Go about your business."

When the man was a safe distance away, Joe faced the three who were clearly outraged at what just happened.

Joe stepped forward, not showing fear. "Never roll a white dude. It brings too much attention from the cops." This wasn't a hard and fast rule, but good enough for what Joe needed say.

The largest of the three stood face-to-face with Joe. "You sayin' we don't go after easy money?"

Joe didn't move an inch. "It won't be easy when the cops are crackin' every black kid on the skull to get information on who stole twelve dollars from some old man comin' home from the grocery store. It's just bad business."

There was a long pause as the four of them stood, not wanting to back down. Joe would usually stand there all day until the others moved first, but not today. He turned and walked away, feeling like something inside of him had changed.

He feared it was compassion, which in the streets would turn to weakness. It was only a matter of time before that weakness cost him both money and his life if he didn't find a way to deal with it.

35

Joe decided to go back home for the day. His mom was surprised when he walked inside. Of course, the kitchen smelled amazing as Shirley began whipping up some sort of mouthwatering creations.

Shirley stirred a pot while looking at her son. "You home? So early? Must miss my cookin'."

Joe smiled and sat down at the small kitchen table. "Somethin' like that."

Shirley continued moving pots around, opening the oven and shoving in a large pan, then closing and returning to her pots on the stove. "My Aunt Mamie taught me to make sweet potato pies when she raised me up in Baxley, Georgia. I had a little stool that I stood on so I could reach the counter top and help her."

Joe shifted in his seat. "Sounds like a good time."

Shirley kept her back to him, stirring another pot. "Well, Aunt Mamie loved me and wanted to show me as much as possible so I would be able to cook on my own."

Joe narrowed his eyes, wondering why his mom was telling this story. "I guess it worked."

Shirley lifted another pan and placed it in the oven. "She taught me how to make biscuits, fried chicken and how to use every ingredient just right so the food tasted like pure love."

Joe smiled. "Now I'm getting hungry."

Shirley turned and wobbled to a chair, eased down and caught her breath. She then gazed at her son. "It just takes the right instruction, the right ingredients, and everything will taste perfect."

Joe reached his hand out and touched hers. "Is there a point?"

Shirley squeezed Joe's hand. "I've been trying to teach you the right ingredients, but it took someone else to find a way to get your attention. I praise God for that and can see the look in your eyes have already soften."

Joe pulled his hand back. "Being soft isn't what I'm about."

Shirley forced herself up and walked to the stove. "There's a difference between soft and being humble. If you were strong enough, you'd know what I mean. I'll wait patiently why you figure it out."

Joe's mouth watered at the smell of everything cooking together. "Is the sweet potato pie almost done?"

Shirley formed a grin. "It's not cookin' you hungry for. An empty stomach is good to find wisdom."

Joe reluctantly stood up. He was going to just walk away, but first he gave his mother a kiss on the cheek. "I'll see ya later."

Joe walked to the door. He indeed felt a hunger like he never felt in his life.

36

Joe climbed into his car and drove. A few minutes later, he ended up at the church Breakstone had taken him.

After sitting in the car for a half hour, Joe finally decided to get out and walk up the stairs to the church door.

Should he knock?

Walk in?

Would they think he's trying to rob the place?

Why was he even here?

Joe turned, looked at the parking lot with four cars, including his. He then turned and faced the doors, reached to the handle and pulled it open.

37

Breakstone hated watching the news on television, listening to the radio, or reading the newspapers. Here's an example of why he came to this decision.

THE KNUCKLEHEAD OF THE DAY AWARD

SARASOTA — Driving with your car stereo too loud can get you a ticket. If Sarasota police have their way it could also get your car impounded and cost you at least $500 to get it back.

Sarasota police want the authority to tow away drivers' cars if they are caught playing the stereo too loud, driving with a suspended license or leaving the scene of a minor crash — all misdemeanor charges.

Sarasota police Lt. Steve Breakstone said towing a car and charging the owner a $500 fine to pick it up is an effective crime-fighting tool that will make people think twice about breaking the law again.

"There are certain people in the community who don't care how many times police arrest them or issue a citation," Breakstone said. "But they care if you impound their car."

(All this made sense to Breakstone, but the person writing the article disagreed.)

Guilty till proven innocent is the mantra of law enforcement across much of the United States. Unless you're a fellow law enforcement. In that case, you'll be given a helping hand after your DUI for driving on the wrong side of the interstate and killing two people.

(Steve raised his hands, "What!")

The articled continued.

Sarasota Police Chief Peter Abbott dismissed any notion that the measure is intended to raise money for the city, pointing out that it is against the law to enact an ordinance to collect revenue. He said expanding his department's ability to impound cars would address 'quality of life' issues, such as noise pollution that residents complain about citywide.

Listen Chief Peter Abbott. If you're police have enough time to arrest people for playing music too loudly, you and your department are overstaffed. Get off your backside, put down those donuts, and start busting real criminals. But before that, I name Sarasota Florida Police Chief Peter Abbott today's Knucklehead of the Day!

38

Breakstone couldn't believe that someone could get away with writing about the police like this and have no consequences or held responsible for their actions.

Did the writer actually call the police chief a Knucklehead??? Not to mention the writer said that towing cars for playing loud music, driving with a suspended license, or leaving the scene of a minor crash is basically okay and Breakstone was a knucklehead for defending his chief.

Breakstone read the comments below. At least ninety percent disagreed with the article and how it was written. (That was a relief.) Some of those who disagreed were daily readers of the website.

Should Breakstone really get upset? Did the comments of people sticking up for police actually make him feel better?

Well, it didn't.

Everyone is entitled to their opinion, but should people get away with slandering police over enforcing laws?

Little did Breakstone know, this was just the beginning…things in the media would one day become much worse.

39

Officer Randy Boyd witnessed a driver going the wrong direction on a one-way street. He called for backup, then pulled the driver over. Breakstone arrived just a few seconds later.

Boyd approached the driver. Meanwhile, Breakstone cautiously approached the passenger side. He heard the driver say his name to Boyd, "David St. Elmos." David had no idea Breakstone was there.

Boyd: "Well Mr. St. Elmos, you were going the wrong direction in a one-way. I'll need your license and registration."

When David reached for the glove compartment, Boyd noticed a bag of marijuana. Boyd stood tall, looking over the roof of the car, and gave Breakstone the signal for "weed."

After David handed Boyd the license and registration, Boyd said, "I'll need you to hand over the bag of marijuana as well."

David: "What?"

Boyd: "The bag of marijuana that's in your pocket. I saw it, so just hand it over."

David reached into his pocket, then pulled his hand up without the bag, and quickly lowered his hand in a different pocket. He attempted to get is .38 revolver, but the handle got stuck on the pocket. Boyd didn't see the gun, but Breakstone saw it from the passenger's side.

Breakstone yelled, "Gun! Gun! Gun!" Randy stumbled back. Breakstone retrieved his weapon and aimed it at David's face. "Do not move. You'll live if you do what I say."

David froze.

Breakstone kept his gun steady. "Don't do anything that I don't tell you to do, or you'll get shot." Randy regained his senses and now had his weapon pointed at David from the driver's side.

Breakstone: "I'm going to walk you through getting the gun out of your pocket. If you do anything I don't tell you, you'll get shot. Place your thumb and finger on the handle and wiggle the gun out of the pocket."

David did as he was told.

Breakstone: "Now, place the gun gently on the passenger's seat."

David complied.

Breakstone: "Lift your hand away from gun and place both of your hands on the steering wheel."

David removed his thumb and finger away from the .38 and gripped the steering wheel. Randy holstered his weapon and handcuffed David.

In court, David St. Elmos told the jury that he had every intention of giving Officer Randy Boyd the .38.

When Breakstone testified, he said, "Yeah right, he was going to give the officer the gun alright…he was going to shoot him."

It was discovered that David had been on probation and knew he was going back to prison. His plan was to shoot Officer Boyd and drive off, but David never knew Breakstone was there, which foiled his plans.

40

Angela Field Willis and Norma "Pearl" Ferreira were both prostitutes in Breakstone's area. They didn't work for Joe, but rather more on their own.

Breakstone thought about what his boss said about busting a prostitute then taking her to church the following Sunday…how would that look? The media would have a field day.

Breakstone had challenged Joe and he ended up in church. Perhaps a similar approach could be used with Angela and Norma.

"God has a different plan for your life," Breakstone told them. "I'm not judging you or condemning you, I'm just saying God has a plan."

The thing was, every woman who ended up in this neighborhood as prostitutes were beautiful. They just had a rough time with life, became addicted to drugs, and the path led them to this profession.

As for Norma, her mother was a prostitute as well and led her daughter into the business.

Norma decided to contact the program, ESTHER. They assisted her with clothing, food, small household items, and connected her to other community resources.

It was explained to Norma, "You are courageous and worthy of hope. Let's not focus on why you're here, or how you arrived in your current situation. Instead, let's focus on today and how to get through this season of your life."

Norma moved to New York. She graduated high school online, then graduated from the Paul Mitchell Academy of Cosmetology, worked at several jobs including hairstyle and bartending, along with going to school for her nursing license.

She sent Breakstone a message saying, "I made it! I got out! You helped me! I'm doing really well. No drug issues and I turned my life around! I'm reading the bible and planting seeds. I know it takes a long time to see results, but I now understand that God sees the results right away and one day the seeds I'm planting will produce, just like it was with me!!!"

Yes indeed, God had a plan.

"Let your eyes look directly forward." ~ Proverbs 4:25

As for Angela Willis, she also contacted Breakstone and said, "All the years you talked to me, you never thought I listened. A lot of people were afraid of you, but didn't know your heart. I was listening. I now live in Michigan, have a family and a job. Thank you for talking to me about God."

In all fairness, Breakstone just told both Norma and Angela that God had a plan for them. He didn't drag them to church, read bible passages to them, or even pray for them.

Whenever he saw them, he just kept saying, "God has a plan for you." Apparently, it's all he had to say.

"Trust in the Lord with all your heart and do not lean on your own understanding. In all your ways acknowledge Him and He will make straight your paths."
~ Proverbs 3:5-6

41

Breakstone had taken it upon himself to lead the attempt of a new anti-prostitution legislation in the state of Florida. He travelled to the State Capital and testified before Legislative Committees, then made a second trip on short notice with little time to prepare.

In addition, Breakstone worked directly with State Attorney Earl Moreland and Chief Justice Bennett on enhancing penalties for prostitution rings near schools and parks. Breakstone made others consider efforts to remove prostitutes from the streets and help women steer in the right direction.

The Sarasota Police Department awarded Breakstone with a Department Commendation for his efforts.

42

Late at night, two black men rushed around the corner to the front door of Tibby's house. One of them was Mark, the younger brother of Joe and Tibby. The other was nicknamed, Tuna, built like a fullback. Both had on football jerseys and jeans, with sweat drizzling down their face.

As they approach the front door, Tuna pulled a pistol from his pocket. Mark knocked on the door yelling, "Tibby! Tibby! Wake up!"

When no one answered, Tuna hurried around the house, looking in windows and knocking on the glass.

Mark became persistent. He banged his fist on the door. "Tibby! Wake up! They after us!"

A porch light suddenly turned on. Tuna ran back to Mark, anxiously waiting for the door to open.

Tibby appeared, wearing a t-shirt and boxers, looking at Tuna shoving the pistol back in his jeans. "What you doin' with that boy? No good come from a gun. You goin' get yourself killed."

Mark slipped by Tibby and entered the house. Tuna tried to do the same thing, but Tibby grabbed him by the arm.

Tibby locked eyes on Tuna as the sweat poured down his face. Tuna yelled, "Let me in!"

"Can't," Tibby said, still holding on to Tuna's arm. "You're not goin' to bring trouble inside this house."

"They after us! After me, after Mark! Let me in!"

"Who's after you?"

"Ebab and Cadillac. Deoley too!"

Tibby let go of Tuna's arm. "What you do?"

"Notin'!"

Tibby sighed. "Go now. Get out of here."

Tuna yelled in the house, "Aunt Marcia! Let me in!"

Tibby kept a level tone. "She's the one who told me not to let you in. Get goin'."

"Ebab going' to kill me." Tuna's voice became shaken. "Mark was there. They'll get him next. Please let me in."

Tibby shouted in the house, "Mark! Come here!"

Mark approached the door.

Tibby asked him, "What really happened?"

Mark glanced at Tuna, then looked at his older brother. "Tuna went to collect some money from Ebab. Things got out of control and Tuna pressed his gun on Ebab's baby while in the crib."

Tibby pulled in a deep breath, glaring at Tuna. "Boy…that was just stupid."

"I know," Tuna pleaded. He looked around. "You goin' let me in?"

"No," Tibby persisted. "Walk away and take your troubles with you."

"What about Mark?"

Tibby looked at Mark. "He's my brother and I'll deal with him." Tibby pointed to the road. "I'm not goin' to tell you again. Go!"

Tuna looked at both Tibby and Mark, hoping for a glimmer of mercy, but none could be found.

The reality was if Ebab arrived with his crew looking for Tuna, everyone would get killed including Mark, Tibby, and even Aunt Marcia.

Tuna stepped off the porch, ran across the street between two houses and disappeared in the darkness.

43

As Tuna ran away, Tibby noticed a slow moving Sedan rounding the corner. Walking next to the Sedan was about twenty thugs. The mob creeped to the house and stopped.

Ebab climbed out of the car, along with Cadillac and Deoley.

Ebab: "Tuna! Mark! We know you're in there! Come out!"

Tibby remained in the doorway. "Tuna not here. I sent him away. To be honest, I let Mark in, but he's not the one you want."

Ebab: "Tell Mark to come out."

Tibby: "You don't want him. You don't want me or Marcia. Find Tuna and take your troubles away from my home."

Cadillac: "You kiddin' us Tibby? If Tuna in it, then Mark in it. Tell him to come out here."

When Deoley moved forward, everyone became dead silent.

Deoley: "We ain't playin'. Get Mark out here."

Tibby felt a drizzle of sweat run down his neck. "Deoley…you in this?"

Deoley: "We all are."

Tibby: "I'm goin' inside. If you got a problem, take it up with Joe. He wouldn't like you comin' to his aunt's house. Just walk away."

Tibby hurried inside the house and locked the door.

The crowd of thugs waited to see what Deoley was going to do next. Cadillac raised his shirt, exposing his nickel plated revolver with a pearl handle. Deoley gazed at the gun, then shifted his eyes to the house.

"Let's go," Deoley said in a low, yet commanding voice. "Now's not the time."

44

Tibby grabbed his cellphone. He debated calling the police, but instead, called the next best thing. He called his brother.

Joe answered, sounding groggy as if he'd been sleeping. "Yeah?"

"It's Tibby. We got a problem."

"What?"

"Tuna went to collect some money from Ebab."

"So?"

"Well, something went wrong and Tuna pointed a gun at Ebab's kid."

"What!" Joe sounded fully awake now.

"He got away and came to my house, bringin' them all here."

"That idiot."

Tibby cleared his throat. "Mark was with Tuna when it all happened."

Joe sighed through the phone. "I'll be right there."

45

It was three o'clock in the morning when Joe arrived. He told Tibby to get in the car and told Mark to stay inside the house.

Joe pulled away while speaking to Tibby. "Is Aunt Marcia alright?"

Tibby rolled his neck. "Yeah. Just pissed that Tuna brought this trouble to the house."

Joe looked in the review mirror. "Mark shouldn't have been with Tuna."

"I know," Tibby said. "Deoley and the rest of the crew are probably at Kingsway, plannin' what to do next."

Joe gripped the steering wheel. "Then that's where we goin'."

46

Still driving, Joe called Burt and Flash. "I need you at Kingsway." He hung up, thinking about what to do next. This was exactly the kind of thing that could spiral out of control. Tuna screwed up big time and now all of them would have to pay the price.

The thing is, there's no negotiating. Ebab won't let this go. Actually, Joe felt Ebab had a case. If someone put a gun to Joe's mother, or his aunt, he would hunt that person down and kill him with his bare hands.

To make things worse, Cadillac was always looking for a reason to kill someone. Deoley was hotheaded and now becoming feared in the neighborhood.

The weakness that Joe had felt, already begun to surface. If Joe was going to make it through the night, he had to be stronger than ever.

47

Joe parked the car. He and Tibby climbed out. Burt and Flash were already there, waiting for them.

Flash lifted his shirt, showing his pistol. "We ready."

Joe shook his head. "If this comes down to a gun battle, we all dead. Keep that thing put away."

Burt formed a cocky grin. "They got guns. We got guns."

Joe glared at him. "Exactly. If we let the guns do the talkin' then no one goin' make it till mornin'."

48

Joe, Tibby, Burt and Flash rounded the corner and marched to Kingsway where they found the Sedan. The twenty gang members were still there, along with Ebab, Cadillac, and Deoley.

Ebab smiled. "Well, well. Look who comin'."

Cadillac handed Ebab the nickel plated pistol. "Here you go. Finish it."

Just as Joe and others were approaching, Tuna flew out of the shadows and ran towards Ebab.

Joe stopped and whispered to himself, "Oh, God…"

Tuna blasted through the crowd with a closed fist, surprised Ebab and punched him in the face. Ebab's cheek burst like a balloon as blood flowed into his shirt.

Ebab fired the pistol, just missing Tuna's ear.

Most of the crowd scattered in different directions. They weren't going to get shot over this, or get arrested.

Tuna grabbed Ebab and wrestled him to the ground. Ebab attempted another shot, but Tuna was able to force Ebab's finger back, almost breaking it as they continued wrestling on the ground.

Cadillac ran off, along with Burt and Flash. They knew this fight was going to end up with someone dead. Although it would be great to see, someone will eventually call the police and everyone remaining in the parking lot will end up in jail.

On the ground, Ebab tried punching Tuna while attempting to point the gun in Tuna's face. Tuna fought back with desperate strength, holding Ebab's arm with one hand and punching him with the other.

Deoley casually walked up and snagged the pistol from Ebab's hand, then fired down at Tuna.

The shot missed and the bullet plugged into the ground.

This caused Tuna to roll off Ebab and run in a full sprint, not looking back.

In seconds, he was gone.

Ebab stood with blood draining down from his cheek. He glared at Deoley for a second, then scampered away.

Tibby pulled at Joe's shirt. "Let's go. It's over."

As Tibby turned, Deoley raised the gun and fired. The bullet exploded into Tibby's back, sending him to the ground.

49

Joe froze with fear, watching Tibby fall to his knees, mouth open, eyes squeezed shut. He dropped forward as blood drained from his back. He clawed his fingers into the concrete, making one desperate attempt to put distance between himself and Deoley.

Suddenly, Tibby stopped moving.

Joe marched towards Deoley. "You shoot him in the back! You ain't a man!"

Deoley raised the pistol. Joe turned to run, but didn't get a step before the gun fired and the bullet hit Joe's spine and exploded out his stomach with a lightning bolt of pain.

Joe collapsed to the ground next to his brother.

Another shot rang out, echoing into the night air. Joe realized the bullet didn't hit him.

Joe rolled to his back, then moved his head to the side, seeing Tibby on his stomach, not moving.

Two more shots were fired. Joe felt the horrific pain of both bullets ripping into his skin and muscles, tearing through his insides.

He reached to his right, attempting to hold Tibby's hand, but he couldn't find him. Seconds passed by as Joe's breathing became ragged and painful. He gazed into the night sky, feeling the world slip away.

The church he had visited became like a vision. He floated inside the doors, down the aisle, approaching the cross.

Joe had given his life to Jesus.

Now, his life had slipped away.

50

It had been a peaceful night. Breakstone had actually been thinking about his kids when the radio came to life, "10-71, shots fired, 27th and Osprey." The dispatcher's voice was calm, but it didn't ease Breakstone's heart which began drumming into his chest.

Breakstone flicked on his lights and stepped on the gas, imagining exactly what he would do once he arrived on the scene. He was the closest officer in the area, so he would be first to assess the situation and take control. He went over his training as he sped down the empty streets.

Park at a safe distance and take cover.

Create a barrier between myself and the gunman.

Draw my gun.

Command that the shooter drop his weapon and lie on the ground.

Breakstone went over in his mind how he would speak to the gunman. The way he spoke to the gunman could be the difference of whether or not shots would be fired in his direction, along with endangering the lives of officers who would arrive shortly after.

Keep my gun in my dominate hand, leaving my other hand free to radio in updates.

If the gunman doesn't follow Breakstone's instructions, or makes a threatening movement, he would have to make a split-second decision.

As Breakstone rounded the corner, he considered it was possible that the suspect was someone he crossed paths with before. This was his area and he knew all the threats.

Despite that, which threat would it be? Who lost their temper tonight?

Breakstone arrived and hit the brakes. Right away he noticed two bodies on the ground. He exited the car, weapon drawn, scanning the area for the gunman.

51

It was obvious the gunman had left the scene. Breakstone updated the dispatcher and hurried to the two bodies, keeping his gun drawn while shifting his eyes in every direction.

The first body was face down. Breakstone crouched down. Suddenly the body moved, turning to the side.

It was Tibby, Joe's brother.

Breakstone moved the second body and kneeled down. He whispered, "Joe…"

Breakstone quickly holstered his weapon and touched Joe's neck, feeling for a pulse.

There wasn't one…Joe was dead.

More officers arrived, filling the night air with red and blue lights.

Breakstone shifted back to Tibby and placed his hand on Tibby's arm. "Who did this?"

A wheezing sound came from Tibby's bloody mouth. He swallowed, then spoke with a tear sliding from his eye. "Deoley."

52

Over the night, every officer was called in to search for Deoley. The morning sun burned into the sky, turning the air hot and humid.

Tibby was in critical condition, but there was a good chance he would make it. Joe had died before Breakstone arrived on the scene.

Breakstone changed his clothes and drove to Shirley's house. He sat in the driveway, trying to think of what he was going to say.

Joe had given his life to Jesus. Why would this happen? How could God take Joe away from this world when God could have used Joe as an example of how anyone, even a gang member, could bring himself to Jesus?

Breakstone climbed out of his car, walked towards the house with his eyes on the doorway. Shirley must have been standing there, waiting for him to approach. She opened the screen door, using her aluminum cane to move onto the porch.

Tears drained from Shirley's eyes. "Is it Joe or Tibby?"

Breakstone walked all the way to her, still unable to find the words.

Shirley gently touched his arm. "Just tell me."

He took in a deep breath. "Both Joe and Tibby were shot last night."

Shirley swallowed. "Are they alive?"

"Tibby is in critical condition, but the doctors think he'll pull through." Breakstone paused. "Joe…"

Shirley lost her grip on the cane and fell to her knees. Breakstone looked up, wanting to ask God for help, but he felt farther away from God than ever before. He dropped to his knees, hugging Shirley.

"I'm sorry." He didn't know what else to say. The words were empty and meaningless.

Shirley cried for several minutes. Then with Breakstone's help, they both rose to their feet. Shirley cleared her throat and asked, "Who did this?"

"A man named, Deoley." Breakstone found his inner strength and said, "I'll do the best I can. From what I heard, he left town."

Shirley reached forward with her trembling fingers and gripped Breakstone's hand. "You don't understand something. God told me that you'll catch him."

Suddenly it was like God's vision transformed from her hand to his, giving Breakstone a clear message. He had let so many other people down in his life and didn't want to gurantee he'd catch Joe's killer, but the impact of God had spoken to her, then to him.

Breakstone took in a deep breath and said, "I'm going to get him. If I have to track him down to the other end of the world, I'm going to get him."

Shirley wiped the tears from her face and whispered, "You brought Joe to Jesus." She lowered her head and repeated, "You brought Joe to Jesus…thank God."

"You were sealed for the day of redemption." ~ Ephesians 4:30

53

Breakstone didn't feel thankful or relieved he brought Joe to Jesus, only to be murdered in a crummy parking lot. In fact, Breakstone resented God for taking Joe's life.

Shirley had prayed every day for Joe to find Jesus. Her prayers were answered, but only to be destroyed by the news her son was killed. What purpose did it serve to save Joe's soul while taking his life at the same time?

As Breakstone drove away, he only had one thought on his mind…

Catch Joe's killer.

A bible verse began to guide his steps. "The greatest love a person can have for his friends is to give his life for them." (John 15:13)

On Breakstone's back, based on that bible verse, he had three words tattooed, "Willing to Die."

Breakstone had put his life on the line every day for the Sarasota Police Department. Now, he was putting his life on the line for Joe.

"In Him we have redemption through His blood, the forgiveness of our trespasses, according to the riches of His grace." ~ Ephesians 1:7

54

For being a streetwise thug, Deoley wasn't very smart. The FBI notified Breakstone that they had tracked Deoley's cellphone and believe he had traveled from Florida to Georgia.

Breakstone met the FBI Special Agent in Charge at Atlanta, where Deoley's cellphone had continued to be tracked. The fear Breakstone had was Deoley could be leading them on a wild goose chase. What if he put the cellphone inside some person's car with Georgia plates?

They could be chasing Deoley to Atlanta, but in reality, he's in Texas or on his way to the west coast.

Breakstone sat in the SUV with the other FBI agents. They had been watching the area by the Atlanta Braves Stadium.

Appearing around the corner was Deoley, talking on his cellphone.

Breakstone had a mix of emotions. He wanted to jump out of the SUV and beat Deoley to death. Despite that, Breakstone also felt justice will be done and Deoley will be sent away for murder, along with many other charges piled on.

He watched as the FBI agents exited the SUV and took Deoley down. Breakstone wanted to be satisfied, but it was difficult.

Instead, Breakstone closed his eyes, thinking of Joe in heaven. Also, Shirley will receive the news that Joe's killer was caught.

There wasn't much else Breakstone could ask for at this point. He opened his eyes, watching Deoley being escorted towards the SUV.

"This is a true saying, to be completely accepted and believed: Christ Jesus came into the world to save sinners...I am the worst of them." ~ 1 Timothy 1:15

55

Redemption means to free someone from bondage. It's also involves paying a price to make the redemption possible.

As Breakstone sat on his bed, he began to wonder if he needed to pay a price for Joe, or for himself. Breakstone felt like he was in bondage and had yet to pay the price for the sins he committed which haunted him every day.

One tear drizzled down Breakstone's face, followed by his eyes blurred with more tears.

He whispered to himself, "Am I loved by anyone?"

Shirley loved her son, Joe. Perhaps as a Christian, she loved all people, including Breakstone. However, it didn't fill the darkness he felt in his soul.

Did he even love himself?

Loneliness began to catch up to Breakstone. He inched forward to the edge of the bed, unable to hold back the tears draining from his eyes. Breakstone then said in an unfamiliar shaken voice, "God if you're real, prove it to me. I want to see it in a real way with no doubt it is You. Here's my one, simple, simple, request. I want to feel real love. I want to know You exist. Please…give me a sign."

Breakstone had been going to church just enough to know you shouldn't put God to the test. However, soon as the word, "sign" came out of Breakstone's mouth, the pager on his belt went off. It was a message from a Christian friend, Linford Sommers.

Breakstone stared at the pager and said to himself, "Oh great, it's Mr. Happy."

56

Sommers was a devout Christian. You could burn this guy's house down and he'll respond by thanking God he had insurance. He would then say something like, "All will be well."

Sommers loves the Lord so much, nothing could separate his faith.

Despite all of that, Breakstone didn't want to talk with him while being in this vulnerable state of mind.

Yet, it seemed as if the pager was gazing at Breakstone, not letting him off the hook. Breakstone reluctantly called him.

Sommers: "Steve, I have to see you right away."

Breakstone: "Really?"

Sommers: "Yes, right away. Right now."

Breakstone: "Well, if you feel that way, come on over."

Breakstone stood, looked in the mirror, seeing the pain on his face. Sommers is a good man and will instantly see how much Breakstone was suffering. In fact, Breakstone believed that Sommers would be able to see every sin

Breakstone committed like a flashing sign dangling above his head.

Every problem Breakstone caused with his wife and kids, the countless wrongs he had done despite attending church, the confusion and emotional suffering over Joe's death, and most of all, the love he hadn't felt from anyone, including himself.

Breakstone wanted to call Sommers back and tell him this wasn't a good time, but knowing Sommers, he would bang on Breakstone's door until it broke down.

"All that the Father gives me will come to me, and whoever comes to me I will never cast out." ~ John 6:37

57

Sommers arrived in quick fashion. Breakstone was still reluctant to answer the door, but he gathered up the strength and just wanted to get this over with. (A mustard of strength.)

Breakstone opened the door and stepped to the side. "Come in." He prepared himself as Linford walked in and locked eyes with him. It seemed if Linford was unveiling Breakstone's soul.

However, that wasn't the case. Linford reached into his pocket and pulled out a piece of paper. "God told me to give this to you."

Breakstone took the piece of paper and held the note like it was the most valuable possession ever given to him.

Sommers then gave Breakstone a quick hug and left.

Breakstone made it back to the side of the bed where he previously prayed to God and asked for a sign of his existence while questioning if anyone loved him.

He lowered his eyes and read the note.

"Tell Steve I LOVE HIM"
I will not allow him to be sifted away from Me.
Tested YES. He must and will be tested. Job was tested. Job was tested and he prevailed.
Tell Steve I love him!!!

Romans 6:5-23, and Chapters 7&8

Breakstone read the note over several more times.

His heart melted and now his eyes drained with tears. He had challenged God and in return, God sent a messenger. Breakstone envisioned God saying, "This knucklehead is about to ask Me to be loved. I need to have a note ready."

So the amazing thing was, Sommers must have thought about writing the note before Breakstone began questioning God and asking if anyone loved him. This meant God was speaking to Sommers before Breakstone began his prayer.

Then God timed it out perfectly so that when Breakstone finished, the pager would ring one second later. Then during the phone call, Sommers would ask to come over so he could personally hand him the note.

Another amazing thing was Sommers had been obedient to God. Think about what had to happen. Sommers was given instructions from God during a random moment at night. Sommers clearly heard the voice of God, obeyed, and had the faith that he was doing the right thing, not knowing that Breakstone was on the edge of his bed, about to make the most important prayer of his life.

God accepted being put to the test and gave Breakstone the sign he was looking for.

Also, God proved to him that he was indeed loved.

Finally, God also showed that He answers prayers before they are even spoken.

58

Breakstone became on fire for the Lord. He began digging into the bible, searching for wisdom and instruction. However, there was just one problem.

Breakstone was still a police officer. How could he use God's wisdom in his job? Breakstone began to think he could apply the teachings of the bible into his everyday life, but he was still the tough guy cop who had a job to do.

His system of playing the tough-guy-Christian worked for a while, but it ended being a path to destruction. God had offered a way for Breakstone to live his life and be a Christian police officer at the same time, but he didn't believe in it, despite the incredible Myracle God had already performed in his life.

It was like the disciples walking with Jesus, yet still frightened during a storm.

They had Jesus right there, but it wasn't enough to still their hearts.

It was true that God proved to Breakstone he was loved, but there was something more important.

Breakstone was to love others.

"Fear not, for I am with you; Be not dismayed, for I am your God. I will strengthen you, Yes, I will help you, I will uphold you with My righteous right hand." ~ Isaiah 41:10

59

There was a time when Breakstone's partner, Officer Perez, made a comment to him when they were walking through a crowd. Breakstone's eyes shifted to each person, looking for anything that could be wrong. He was evaluating based on instinct and experience, getting a sense if something bad was about to happen.

Perez: "I've never seen anyone with your ability."

Breakstone kept his eyes forward, searching the crowd. "What does that mean?"

Perez: "I have no idea what you're looking at, but I guess you'll know when you see it."

Breakstone smiled. He could pick out a guy in the crowd with a gun, or dope. Over the years, it just became habit.

Despite that, it's not just finding the criminal, but the best way to approach and arrest him, especially in a crowd.

One time when Breakstone noticed a deal going down in a sea of people, he approached and said, "Who's playing the radio loud?"

Everyone would look at him while thinking, "Radio? No one's playing a radio."

The distraction was just enough for him to surprise the drug dealer and grab his arms.

Breakstone would say something like, "You can go to jail, or you can go to jail sweaty…it's up to you."

No one ever fought back.

With Perez complimenting him, it was certainly a nice thing to hear from a fellow police officer. However deep down in Breakstone's soul, he wished there were other areas of his life he could be in control the same way while using his instincts.

Perez's compliment was nice, but Breakstone would rather hear how devoted he was to Jesus Christ; you could pick Breakstone out of a sea of people and see his love for God.

That was his prayer.

60

Breakstone was sleeping in the spare bedroom and Angela in the master bedroom.

Angela had her temperament and Breakstone had his infidelity, so neither was perfect. However, they did have something strange in common…

Throughout their marriage, both continued seeing the numbers, 11-11.

Wherever they went, it seemed like 11-11 kept popping up. On the television. Noticing it on the clock. On a restaurant bill.

Both Angela and Breakstone agreed it had some sort of meaning, but neither of them could figure it out.

As their marriage continued to erode, it seemed less valuable for them to find the meaning of the 11-11, until tonight, when Angela was in a deep sleep. She woke at two in the morning and screamed, "Steve! Come here!"

Breakstone hurried to the master bedroom, thinking there had been an intruder. "What's wrong?"

Angela was sitting up in the bed. "I know what it means! I know what eleven-eleven is!"

Breakstone sat on the bed next to her. "How do you know?"

"God told me it's the eleventh book of the bible and the eleventh chapter."

Breakstone left the room, grabbed a bible from the desk drawer, then raced back to the spare bedroom. He counted eleven books of the bible and ended up on 1 Kings. He then quickly turned to 1 Kings and began reading the eleventh chapter.

It discussed King Solomon, who married women that he should have stayed away from because they would tempt him to worship other gods. God had warned Solomon of this, but to no avail.

Solomon married 700 princesses and had 300 concubines.

What God had warned Solomon about had come true. While Solomon had more wisdom, wealth and power than any of the kings before him, he drifted from the Lord. *"Solomon followed Ashtoreth the goddess of the Sidonians, and Molek the detestable god of the Ammonites." (1 Kings 11:5)*

Breakstone read the passage again, then stared at the floor, lost in thought. Solomon and the other women worshiped gods including the goddess Ashtoreth.

Ashtoreth.

Ashtoreth.

Suddenly a flood of memories returned back to when Breakstone was in eleventh grade and found the bloody note in his locker.

The strange thing is, he never told Angela about the note. Fast-forward all those years later and she's having a vision from God which led Breakstone to 1 Kings Chapter 11.

Breakstone thought about the note written in blood, remembering exactly what it had said…

STAY AWAY FROM HER. SHE CAN NEVER LOVE YOU LIKE I CAN. WE WERE MEANT TO BE TOGETHER.

61

After taking all this in, Breakstone looked down at the bible and read 1 Kings, 11:4. "As Solomon grew old, his wives turned his heart after other gods and his heart was not fully devoted to the LORD his God, as the heart of David, his father, had been."

This passage was a clear message to Breakstone; originally given to him when he was in eleventh grade. Breakstone's heart was not fully devoted to the Lord.

When Solomon's heart was lost, God compared it to David. *"God said, 'I have found David son of Jesse, a man after my own heart. He will do everything I want him to do.'" (Acts 13:22)*

Was Breakstone a, "Man after God's own heart?"

To fully understand, Breakstone had to know what it meant to be a person devoted to God's heart.

It meant being humble…Breakstone was arrogant.

Trusting…Breakstone had become a man who couldn't be trusted as a husband, no better than Solomon tempted by other women and led astray.

Loving…Breakstone loved his family, including his soon to be ex-wife. However, his love would always be tainted until he put God first in his life.

Devoted…Breakstone was devoted to his job and his own personal ambitions, but not fully devoted to God.

Recognition….Breakstone never gave God the credit for his success. Instead, it was Breakstone who was the "superman" in his own life. He believed God to be distant, in which he further believed that he had full control over his life when it was actually unraveling.

Faithfull…Breakstone had faith in himself, not in God's plans for his life.

Most of all, redemption. Breakstone was not being saved from temptation or regaining possession of his actions by dedicating his heart to God's heart.

Breakstone recalled the librarian telling him, "It's a curse," then said the name, "Ashtoreth." Now years later, Breakstone was reading this in the eleventh book of the bible and the eleventh chapter.

The question then became, "What else did the bible say about Ashtoreth?"

62

"Once again, the Israelites sinned against the Lord by worshiping the Baals and the Astartes (Ashtoreth)…they abandoned the Lord and stopped worshiping Him." ~ Judges 10:6

This was yet another verse stating how people abandoned the Lord and placed their heart with the goddess Ashtoreth. Was Ashtoreth a distraction created by Satan? Or was Ashtoreth formed by worldly men and women, then grew into something powerful based solely on legend?

"We will offer sacrifices to our goddess, the Queen of Heaven (Ashtoreth), and we will pour out wine offerings to her. Then we will have plenty of food, we will prosper, and have no troubles." ~ Jeremiah 44:17

The women baked cakes shaped like the Queen of Heaven, offered sacrifices to her, and poured wine offerings to her. Their husbands approved of this.

What's even more disturbing is how easily men went along with this and even helped. The original example was Solomon. He had more power and wisdom than anyone, but a few women mentioned Ashtoreth, which caused Solomon to become powerless to stop them. In fact, he spent time and resources to help worship Ashtoreth.

Despite many people worshiping Ashtoreth and placing their hope in this goddess, their lands became ruins and they were cursed, because the Lord could no longer endure their wicked ways and evil practices. By offering sacrifices to Ashtoreth and making promises to her, they no longer had the favor of the Lord. (Jeremiah 44:15-25)

Breakstone thought about this…cursed. That's was the librarian warned would happen from the note.

Even so, the answer to why the note written in blood was placed in the locker had yet to be explained. Was Ashtoreth real and placed the note in the locker? Did God place the note there as a warning?

The answer had to be in the bible…

63

When the Israelites lost the battle to the Philistines, King Saul, his servant, and Saul's three sons fled. The Philistines caught up with the three sons and killed them.

King Saul had been hit with arrows and was badly wounded. He told his young servant, "Draw your sword and kill me, so that these godless Philistines won't gloat over me and then kill me."

However the young servant couldn't do it, so King Saul threw himself on his own sword. The servant saw what his king had done and did the same.

The Philistines cut off King Saul's head and placed his weapons in the temple dedicated to the goddess Ashtoreth.

For twenty years, the Israelites cried to the Lord for help. Samuel said to the people of Israel, "If you are going to turn to the Lord with all your hearts, you must get rid of all the foreign gods and the images of the goddess Ashtoreth. Dedicate yourselves completely to the Lord and worship only Him, and He will rescue you…" So the Israelites destroyed their idols and worshiped only the Lord. (1 Samuel 7:2-4)

Breakstone thought this was interesting, because the indication of turning away from idols and giving the Lord all your heart was mentioned yet again. This was a pattern that certainly could not be ignored.

In 2 Kings 23:14, it says, "King Josiah broke the symbols of the goddess Ashtoreth. The ground where they had stood he covered with human bones."

Should Breakstone have destroyed that bloody note when he first discovered it was a curse? Did he even believe in curses?

He had only been in eleventh grade and was listening to the advice of adults. First the librarian explained what was so terrible about the note. Then the principal called the police and the note was taken, but nothing ever happened after that day. The police never called him back, nor did Breakstone ever mention the note to anyone.

Until…Angela had a vision from God.

Did it even matter at this point? Of course it did!

A curse is intended to inflict harm on someone. However, that harm comes from supernatural powers.

64

Breakstone once again thought about the note when he first discovered it in his locker.

STAY AWAY FROM HER. SHE CAN NEVER LOVE YOU LIKE I CAN. WE WERE MEANT TO BE TOGETHER.

Breakstone kept replaying the words in his mind. "Stay away from her."

Who should he have stayed away from? His girlfriend in high school? His abusive mother? His future wife?

Perhaps God was warning Breakstone to stay away from Ashtoreth? The note would then read, "Stay away from Ashtoreth. She can never love you like I can. You were meant to be with God."

Based on the other bible passages he read, this made sense. Thousands of people, including powerful kings like Solomon were led astray by this goddess. They began calling her the Queen of Heaven, as if she had just as much love and compassion as God.

When it was all said and done, no one received love or compassion from

Ashtoreth. In fact, they suffered because of their lack of faith in God.

They had become cursed.

Which leads to one more question…

Why did Breakstone and his wife continue seeing the numbers 11-11?

65

Satan had taken everything in Breakstone's life that was good and twisted it just a bit to lead him away from God.

To accomplish this, Satan copies God. The note was a perfect example. It was a message from God, warning Breakstone that he would fall adrift and move farther and farther away from God. Breakstone's reason for this since high school was simple…he didn't need God.

Plenty of people before him felt the same way. They could supplement with their own creation of Ashtoreth, their new Queen of Heaven.

If God was the one to leave that note in the locker when Breakstone was in eleventh grade, then it was God attempting to gain Breakstone's attention. After all, it was written in blood!

Nevertheless, Satan took the situation and twisted it so that Breakstone would actually be drawn to Ashtoreth and become what other people had done, even if it wasn't his original intention.

By Satan accomplishing this plan, God was pushed out of the picture.

So over the years, Breakstone and Angela continued to see the numbers 11-11. This was God attempting to regain Breakstone's attention and bring him to a better place in his life.

Suddenly, his wife had the vision from God, leading Breakstone to 1 Kings Chapter eleven.

But why not give the vision directly to Breakstone?

There are two reasons. First, Breakstone had been ignoring God. He wasn't listening to the Holy Spirit, wisdom, or even bloody notes.

Second, women in the biblical times were able to lead powerful men like Solomon astray. Despite that, women can also lead men to God.

Even though Breakstone and Angela would soon be divorced, he listened when she explained her vision from God. This opened the gates of wisdom for

Breakstone to see the meaning of the numbers 11-11 more clearly.

66

11-11 is actually a beautiful thing. Imagine each person is represented by a column. When you form a relationship with someone, the columns are put close together. There's a space, then a close relationship is formed with another two people.

These relationships (columns) are strong when standing up straight with confidence. *"For where two or more come together in my name, I am there with them." ~ Matthew 18:20*

However, if they are slightly titled, the column loses strength and the entire structure begins to fall apart. Consider all the relationships Satan attempts to breakup. The best way is to make relationships with others improper, which causes them to lose strength.

Breakstone felt that he, along with other Christians, belong between the two sets of columns where it's the best place to operate.

"Let us be concerned for one another, to help one another, to show love and to do good. Let us not give up the habit of meeting together, as some are doing. Instead, let us encourage one another…" ~ Hebrews 10:24-25

Breakstone wanted to find those sets of columns and help people express love and guide others to do good. He wanted sets of people to get back into the habit of meeting in church and in small groups, because so many, like him, had drifted away.

Over the years, Breakstone had been searching for the meaning behind 11-11. However, God would not provide the answer, because Breakstone was looking for meanings behind two numbers (Eleven and Eleven) rather than the notion of God waving His hands in attempt to gain Breakstone's attention.

For example, when Breakstone noticed 11:11 on the clock, it meant nothing except its relation to time.

Numbers were created to give humans organization. Based on that fact, people could always find 11-11 in many ways, but what would it really mean?

Jesus Christ-Our Redeemer. (11 letters -11 letters.)

Jesus is Lord- God in Heaven. (11 letters -11 letters.)

Savior Jesus-God Almighty. (11 letters -11 letters.)

World War I ended at the 11th hour of the 11th day. (Oh, and on the 11th month.)

The 11:11 seen by Breakstone and Angela didn't have some deep meaning. God was just trying to move Breakstone away from his old ways into a new path, which ended up as a vision given to him by Angela.

67

Note to Reader: During Steve Breakstone's interview for this book, he discovered the company who would publish his book was called, Brand Eleven Eleven. Also, the author who helped Breakstone write the book was married on November 11th.

During the interview, when Breakstone was told about the publisher and author, he glanced up at heaven and gave God a moment of praise.

The author then told Breakstone, "Never have any doubts about this book. God just made that clear."

68

In 1 Corinthians 11:11, it says, "In our life of the Lord, woman is not independent of man, nor is man independent of woman." This is saying that people depend on each other. In-between people can be either God, or Satan, like being placed between two sets of columns. One brings strength, the other brings weakness.

God had always been whispering to Breakstone in attempt to pass on His wisdom, which God does for us all. This wisdom finally arrived, but it had to arrive in steps, which looking back, was a battle Breakstone was having in his heart where both God and Satan had their say.

Breakstone found a note written in blood. This was from God, warning Breakstone that he would drift away.

However, Satan twisted that truth just slightly and Breakstone was led to believe the note was a curse.

Years passed, Breakstone became a devoted police officer, devoted father, but lacked in devotion when it came to his wife. Also, Breakstone had virtually no relationship with God, which pleased Satan.

Breakstone, along with his wife, continued to see the numbers 11-11. They both prayed, but the answer would not come. The truth was there, but twisted slightly so they both saw numbers, like the time on a clock.

Breakstone's wife was given a vision by God. This could have easily been twisted again, but this time, Breakstone referred to the bible as his wife instructed.

God continued to give Breakstone wisdom, driving Satan farther away in his life.

Breakstone now believes in his purpose. He had become a man after God's own heart and wants to help others stand up straight and never tilt away from God's love.

Distractions like the goddess Ashtoreth will always be around, because Satan takes what is good, like the phrase God in Heaven and twists it slightly into Queen of Heaven, leading people away from God and into destruction.

There's a 500 year old painting by Raphael called St. Michael Vanquishing Satan, depicting life's battle of fighting evil and giving the power for Michael to step on the devil's neck.

"And God, our source of peace, will soon crush Satan under your feet." - Romans 16:20

Evil attacks, we battle, resist, succumb, God embraces us, Satan still finds a way in, we struggle to get back to God, and the cycle seems to continue.

For Breakstone, the goal was to embrace God and protect himself from people who attempted to drain him with their sinful ways. When fighting evil, there's always someone who will win and someone who will lose. It comes down to understanding how to let God make the decisions.

Now that Breakstone has been given this wisdom, he can place his foot on Satan's neck and draw from God's power to make it difficult for others to go to hell.

"Now war arose in heaven, Michael and his angels fighting against the dragon. And the dragon and his angels fought back, but he was defeated, and there was no longer any place for them in heaven." - Revelation 12:7-8

Satan gains access into our heart by using lies. When Breakstone suddenly felt loved and even blessed to be closer than ever to God, that's when Satan once again began to attack Breakstone where it would hurt the most.

It was the same with Joe. Satan lied to Joe for many years, convincing him that being a gang leader in a neighbor was more important than being a fishermen of men.

When Satan lies, there's always a common theme.

The first lie is the most important…**Satan doesn't exist.** Breakstone had gone through so much trouble attempting to find love and the presence of God that he didn't realize Satan was always there, hiding in the background, giving Breakstone false information.

As for Joe, God never existed on the streets full of drug dealers, thieves, and gangs. This lie had led Joe away from church and to the business of his neighborhood.

This led to the second lie by Satan…**God is holding back from you.** Breakstone felt God was holding back His love. Breakstone then wanted to know if God really existed. If so, why was God holding back?

The truth was, God was never holding back. It was Breakstone who put the wall up between himself and God.

God never held back from Joe either. There was always Shirley, Joe's mom, praying for her son. There was also Breakstone, an unlikely servant of God, challenging Joe to attend church.

God even used Angela, a soon to be ex-wife to lead Breakstone in the right direction. God never holds back. We hold ourselves back.

In a third lie, Satan did a great job lying to Breakstone that God cannot be trusted. This gave Breakstone the illusion that he had to be Superman. The lie by Satan also gave Breakstone a false sense of courage, which could easily be destroyed.

Joe also had to be Superman in his neighborhood. God wasn't going to stop the bullets. This was proven up to the day Joe died. However, God could be trusted by giving Joe the strength to find Jesus before Joe's last breath was taken.

With that, Breakstone was lied to by Satan once again, being told that sin carries no consequences. Breakstone vowed to uphold the law as a police officer, but forgot his vows as a husband. He also broke God's Commandments as if there was never going to be a problem living life by disobeying God's Law.

Sin did carry consequences for Breakstone as it did for Joe. They didn't have to be perfect, but they did have to recognize God's Commandments and become an example to others.

Satan lied to Breakstone by saying **you can be like God**. This didn't mean Breakstone felt he was a god, but rather he could propel through life without God's presence. "God was for weaker people."

Of course, that was a big lie. Breakstone and Joe didn't have the power to control their own lives without God leading the way.

Finally, Satan lied to Breakstone by saying **if it feels good, then do it**. Breakstone felt invincible, but also had this sense of whatever feels good he should be able to have, even if it hurts others, or hurt himself. (In many ways, it was both.)

Joe lived these lies by Satan, along with people like Ebab, Cadillac, and the man who murdered Joe… a rising star in the streets named Deoley.

All those people Breakstone had arrested were given the same lies. Every day, a whisper from Satan would remind them…

Evil doesn't exist.

God is holding back from you.

God can't be trusted.

Sin and crime carries no consequences.

You can be a god in the streets.

If it feels good, then do it.

Joe fought these lies when he first entered a church. At the same time, Breakstone also had to fight off the lies of Satan.

Despite that, with Joe gone and Breakstone still searching for meaning in his life, love would be the first step to succeeding in God's plan. There couldn't be another way.

As for now, Breakstone's journey would be tested with the only thing he had left…

Being a police officer.

Unfortunately, things were about to get much worse.

"Now the snake was the most cunning animal that the Lord God had made." - Genesis 3:1

70

In 1992, Breakstone was named **SWORN EMPLOYEE OF THE QUARTER** during the months between January and March, then was named, **OFFICER OF THE YEAR**, quickly rising to the top of the police department.

However, Breakstone's relationship with his wife, soon to be ex-wife, certainly caused many problems, which escalated into an uncontrollable brushfire of lies and hatred which Breakstone could not put out.

Angela still lived a few doors down from Breakstone and he still cared for her. They exchanged text messages and even began to flirt again, although, it was all over a cellphone.

As for being a police officer, Breakstone was in the process of retiring. He wanted to do something else with his life. He had a vision of building a church, possibly in Colombia where he could bring people to God just like he did with Joe.

The leadership at Sarasota Police adored Breakstone, including the captains. It certainly made it difficult to completely leave the police department. So instead of retiring, Breakstone was given a certificate to continue working part time as an officer. This was fine, because it gave him a chance to slowly adjust his life and discover what the next move would be.

Then suddenly, it felt like the entire world had turned on him.

71

Angela secretly met with Breakstone's captain and complained he was being violent towards her. She showed the captain text messages of Breakstone making sexual advances. (Keep in mind, these were flirtatious messages in which she sent to him as well.)

The conversation then turned to how Breakstone was acting unusual, possibly becoming unraveled and now threating her physically, including using a gun.

Of course, Breakstone's captain couldn't ignore such a detailed accusation.

When he questioned Breakstone about it, he told the truth and said that none of it happened. There was an explanation for the text messages and an explanation for the gun, which was he gave Angela a gun to protect herself from a hitman who had been after Breakstone.

Also, Breakstone knew his wife wanted more money. He was going to give it to her, but the details hadn't been worked out yet. It appeared she became impatient, or worried that he would change his mind, so for some reason, she figured this would be the best route to take.

This brought on an investigation, headed up by an Internal Affairs officer who didn't think much of Breakstone. (We will call him, Brian.)

When Brian was an officer, he ruthlessly kicked a defenseless homeless guy. (Brian was nicknamed, "Bootsy.") Then later when he headed up S.W.A.T., he did "Underwear checks," because he wanted his men to all be in the same uniform.

There was a time when Breakstone was a shift commander and he heard a call come over the radio about someone who had been beaten up in a bar. Breakstone responded to the emergency, but was later reprimanded by Brian who felt Breakstone broke policy.

Of course, there wasn't a policy, but Breakstone was given a cautionary letter on a rule that never existed. At the same time, Brian looked to change the policy to further punish Breakstone.

Now, Brian was in charge of Breakstone's investigation for abusing Angela.

72

The investigation made Breakstone look like a cop who got his jollies beating his wife. If that was true, then Breakstone certainly would have been fired.

When the investigation brought up an incident that he broke Angela's nose, it was an example of how far off track Internal Affairs had gone while believing his wife's stories.

The truth was that fifteen years ago, the police were called to the home after Angela made a 911 call. She claimed Breakstone had been hitting her. A police report was written and filed, which stated Breakstone did not harm his wife. In fact, Angela was the one being violent.

No charges were filed, or arrests made.

In the final Internal Affairs judgment, they gave Breakstone forty-five days prospective suspension which would begin fifteen days following the filing of the final order.

However, the suspension didn't make sense because Breakstone was basically retired. He wasn't on the daily schedule and didn't have any specific responsibilities. In fact, he was supposed to take a class to reinstate his certificate, but he had no intention because he was finished being a police officer.

Despite that, it looked like Breakstone was suspended from his job for wife abuse.

Breakstone was given one year probation to begin at the conclusion of the suspension, but once again, there was nothing to suspend Breakstone from, because he was a retired police officer and there was no need for probation because he hadn't plan on un-retiring.

The most frustrating thing was Breakstone proved he didn't abuse his wife, yet, Internal Affairs felt it was still necessary for the suspension and probation.

Once again, if Breakstone had been an active police officer and he was found guilty of these crimes, he wouldn't have been suspended…he would have been fired.

And yet, Internal Affairs kept piling it on. They said he would have to complete a commission approved ethics training course prior to the end of the probationary period. Breakstone would also have to complete an officer fitness for duty evaluation prior to re-employment.

"What employment? I'm retired!"

Internal Affairs completed their "punishment" by stating the charges of giving a false statement were dismissed.

Breakstone had never lied, never given a false statement, so there was nothing to dismiss.

It would be like a teacher telling a high school graduate, "You never cheated on a test, so I'm going to put in your record that we dismissed all claims of you cheating, however, you'll still be suspended from school even though you've graduated. If you want to come back to high school for some reason, you'll have to take a special test."

Nothing from Angela's accusations were proven, because there was nothing to prove. Breakstone figured he wasn't a police officer anymore, so there wasn't much damage done. His divorce was finalized and it was now time to move on with his life.

Nevertheless, he forgot about one thing…

The media.

73

When Breakstone read the article by Lee Williams, he couldn't believe his eyes.

"A Sarasota police lieutenant who had been on administrative leave since his ex-wife was granted a protection order against him has retired, just as an internal affairs investigation concluded he violated departmental rules and stalked the woman."

Breakstone stopped and reread certain parts of the article.

Protection order.

Violated department rules.

Stalked a woman.

(Article continued.) "The police department's internal affairs investigators found Lt. Steven Breakstone had violated the department rule requiring officers to obey state laws, specifically the stalking statute, that he engaged in conduct unbecoming an officer and that he was dishonest.

"The State Attorney's Office has declined to file any criminal charges. Breakstone's ex-wife told prosecutors she did not want to involve her children in the case any further. She signed a waiver of prosecution, which stopped the filing of formal charges."

This was all completely twisted around to make Breakstone look bad. He wasn't "unbecoming of an officer" and he certainly wasn't, "dishonest."

What if people in church read this? His family? Friends? What would they think? There were not charges to file and there wasn't a case because his ex-wife wasn't honest and it was proven she lied.

He continued reading.

"The department will now forward its investigation to the Florida Department of Law Enforcement, which could revoke Breakstone's certification."

There wasn't a certificate to revoke because Breakstone was retired and he never intended on taking the classes to renew his certificate!

(Article continued.) "Breakstone, 47, declined to comment. Breakstone and his wife divorced in July 2011. The Sarasota Police Department put Breakstone on administrative leave in January after his ex-wife filed a petition for a protection order.

"During the hearing for the protective order Breakstone's ex-wife said Breakstone had been physically abusive toward her during the marriage, including head-butting her when she was three months pregnant with their second child, breaking her nose."

That incident happened fifteen years ago and it was proven that he didn't break her nose. Not only that, a report was written on how she was the one being violent, not him!

(Article continued with a statement from his ex-wife.) "'Steve's obsession has become terrifying especially now that I have reported him and knowing how unpredictable he is. I live every day in fear.'

"When a judge granted her request for a one-year injunction, Breakstone was ordered to surrender his firearms to the Sarasota County Sheriff's Office."

Breakstone knew the statement, "I live every day in fear," would attract more media attention. It was a perfect way to destroy a police officer's reputation.

He continued reading, now feeling sad, rather than angry.

"Sarasota Police Lt. Steven Breakstone also could soon face a criminal stalking charge for what a Sarasota County Sheriff's Office investigator called, 'Escalating bizarre behavior' since his divorce became final in July."

Breakstone quickly wrote back to the journalist saying, "This is a private matter that should have been dealt with within the family. I still love my ex-wife and I love my children, and I forgive her."

Breakstone wondered how all this would affect his three children. How would people look at him now that the media has begun to bash him?

The true souls in his life have no mask. They are wide open to see their good and their bad. However, what Breakstone was beginning to realize was the Darth Vader's of his life will be disguised as friends, family, or false personas.

This was just the beginning…

74

SARASOTA POLICE OFFICER ACCUSED OF STALKING EX-WIFE

SARASOTA – "A longtime Sarasota Police lieutenant has been put on administrative leave amid allegations that he is stalking his ex-wife, entering her home when she was not there and sending her numerous explicit text messages.

"Lt. Steven Breakstone also could soon face a criminal stalking charge for what a Sarasota County Sheriff's Office investigator called 'escalating bizarre behavior' since his divorce became final in July.

"The Sarasota Police Department put Breakstone on administrative leave Saturday, two days after his ex-wife Angela filed a restraining order petition that includes what she says are nude photos of himself he sent to her.

"A sheriff's office detective who investigated the matter said in a memo that he found probable cause that Breakstone had committed a misdemeanor, and said he will file the charge with the State Attorney's Office in the near future. Prosecutors would then decide if charges should be filed.

"But Breakstone, who has had several contentious disciplinary battles in his 25-year career at the department, said he intends to clear his name after a hearing Friday where he insists the full story will come out."

75

Breakstone looked up from the article. It's always been easy for the media to say things like, "contentious disciplinary battles in his 25-year career at the department."

If someone pulled a police officer's entire file, there's a list of commendations and awards, along with complaints and grievances that had been exonerated, and charges sustained based on no evidence.

With that information, a journalist will look past the commendations and awards, then focus on the complaints and grievances. However, if the journalist understood how things work, they wouldn't print things like, "Eighty-seven complaints of excessive force."

When an officer has a high amount of complaints, especially excessive force, the officer most certainly works in the worst of neighborhoods and is constantly making felony arrests. Also, this officer is the most experienced, since the neighborhood is much more dangerous.

Compare this to an officer that has zero complaints, their area has almost no crime. Also, the officer may go his entire career without making one felony arrest.

It's not saying one officer is better than another. Both do their job, but like any job, there are people who are placed in more difficult areas with the most problems and people who are placed in easier areas.

When Breakstone continued to pile on the felony arrests, he also received complaints from gang members, drug dealers, rapists, and other scum that were trying to find a quick solution to not going to prison.

Although all the complaints were dropped, they have to be filed. This then becomes fuel for a journalist who wants to hurt a police officer's reputation.

For example when Breakstone responded to a spouse battery call, a female neighbor intervened. Several times Breakstone asked for her to leave the porch, but she became angrier and even advanced towards the other woman.

At this point, Breakstone had no choice; he escorted her off the porch.

Of course, the woman filed a complaint. Witnesses were interviewed and Breakstone was exonerated.

On another occasion, Breakstone received twelve stiches on his chin when he was attacked with a broken bottle during an arrest. Guess who made the complaint?

Well it wasn't Breakstone…it was the guy who attacked him.

These are just a few examples of complaints made by people in which Breakstone had to deal with on a daily basis.

76

(Article continued.) "Breakstone invited the sheriff's office detective who investigated the claims, Detective (Brian), to a hearing on the petition Friday.

"'I'm going to go the hearing and give my version of what happened, and prove there's been no violence,' Breakstone said.

"Angela Breakstone said in her petition that her fear of her ex-husband — who lives only about three houses away — has escalated since the divorce, claiming he has tracked her movement, threatened her and badgered people around her.

"This is her second petition for protection; she said the first one in December 2010 was not granted because Steve Breakstone has been friends with the judge for more than 20 years. This time, two judges who were former prosecutors have recused themselves from hearing the case.

"'Steve's obsession has become terrifying, especially now that I have reported him and knowing how unpredictable he is, I live every day in fear,' Angela Breakstone wrote.

"Steve Breakstone, one of four shift commanders who oversee three sergeants and all patrol operations, has told sheriff's investigators that he has strong religious beliefs that are guiding him to try to reunite with his ex-wife.

"He said he is most worried about how the restraining order petition and its contents will affect his three children, ages 10 to 14.

"'It's private a matter that should have been dealt with within the family,' Steve Breakstone said. 'I still love my ex-wife and I love my children, and I forgive her.'

"According to Angela Breakstone, her ex-husband's continued feelings for her are the root of the problem. He has appeared unannounced at her home, watering plants on her porch and bringing plates of food, according to the petition.

"Just like any domestic dispute, however, there are two sides to these stories.

"In her petition, Angela Breakstone submitted text messages from her ex-husband during a time of consensual interaction.

"In a Dec. 30 incident, Angela Breakstone says her daughter caught Steve Breakstone inside her home, going through drawers. He told the girl that the front door had been open and he wanted to make sure a burglar was not inside."

77

Breakstone couldn't believe what he was reading in this badgering article.

First of all if Angela feared Breakstone, why did she move just three doors down? It was the other way around…she wanted to stay close to Breakstone.

As for appearing unannounced at her home, she was referring to one day when Breakstone was driving home from work and saw her front door wide open and a bike out front. There had been some robberies in the neighborhood and witnesses claim they were riding on bikes.

Breakstone called Angela several times while sitting out front watching the house. She didn't answer. Also, the door of the house remained open and no one came in or out.

Breakstone called his daughter, Shalom, several times, but she didn't answer either.

After sitting in the car, debating what to do, he decided to go inside. He raised his gun, announced himself at the door and cautiously walked in. He then checked every room and cleared the house.

Suddenly, Shalom appeared at the doorway. Breakstone holstered his gun and asked her, "Where were you? I tried calling?"

"Sorry, dad. I was at the house."

"Whose bike is out front?"

"It's my friend's."

He shook his head. "You left the door wide open to your mother's house, not to mention you didn't answer your cellphone."

Shalom lowered her head. "Sorry dad."

He patted her on the shoulder. "It's okay. Just…don't leave doors wide open, especially if you're not going to be there."

The reporter never asked Breakstone about Angela's accusations of him walking into her house and checking up on her. Instead, the truth was buried. The incident of him checking for a robbery ended up making him look like a stalking ex-husband.

78

(Article continued.) "On Jan. 14, Angela Breakstone said he came to her home uninvited and questioned her, insulting her guests in the driveway."

The article made Breakstone look like he came over while she was having a party, forced himself inside the house and started yelling at guests.

Actually, here's what really happened…

Breakstone, wearing a t-shirt, pajama bottoms and slippers, had walked over from his home to pick up his son Gabe at Angela's house because no one was answering the phone. Breakstone decided to wait in the driveway for his son after noticing Angela was having a party.

Two guys, both weighing over 275 pounds and built like offensive linemen, appeared from the house and headed to the driveway. One was wearing a brown leather jacket and the other a gray hoodie. Both were arguing about the party, claiming it was boring and a waste of their time.

They both looked at Breakstone, seeing he was wearing pajama bottoms and assumed he lived there.

"That party sucked," Leather Jacket yelled.

Breakstone raised his hands in a defensive position. "Sorry, I don't know anything about it."

Leather Jacket inched forward. "Hey, Joystick, you got a problem?"

That's when Gabe walked outside, saw what was happening and hid behind the bushes.

Everyone from the party suddenly poured out from the house, including Angela, to see what was happening. Breakstone glanced at Gabe. His head poked from the bushes then ducked back down.

Suddenly, Gray Hoodie blindsided Breakstone with a concrete block, striking Breakstone in the back of the head. He fell to one knee, as the world spun around and hot, searing pain ripped through his skull. Also, blood began pouring from his ear for some reason.

Leather Jacket and Gray Hoodie must have took off, because when Breakstone regained his vision, they were gone.

He heard Angela say to Gabe, "Don't tell anyone this happened, especially the police." Angela then repeated this to other people in the party, specifically one of their close friends.

Breakstone drove himself to the hospital. The doctor brought in the police and Breakstone filed a report. (Which the journalist of the article could have easily pulled up.) In the police report, the officer wrote, "Mild injuries." The reason officers sometimes do this is because it saves them time from running a full investigation for assault, or even worse, attempted murder.

It's not the fault of the officers. If Breakstone wanted to push the issue, they would have filed a different report.

After the doctor examined Breakstone, he indeed had a major injury and was lucky to be alive. The doctor said, "No sense in giving you an X-Ray and putting radiation in your brain."

Breakstone actually smiled. It summed up his entire day.

79

(Article continue.) "On Jan. 15, Angela says Steve Breakstone saw her driving in traffic with a male friend, so Breakstone pulled a U-turn to pull up next to her car and yell at her."

Breakstone laughed. This article was a joke. Here's what really happened…

After fishing with Gabe and Shalom at mote marine, they piled into the car, drove through the lot and sat at the red light.

A car pulled up next to them. It was Angela and chiropractor named Sam, who was married and known for being a womanizer. Sam had been going after Angela for many years.

It had gotten so bad, Breakstone had approached Sam at Starbucks and said to him, "You know my wife pretty well. Can you please stay away from her?"

Now this married guy was in the car with Angela while Breakstone and the two kids were in the other car. It was awkward to say the least, but even more, Breakstone's blood boiled when seeing Angela and Sam together.

Breakstone rolled down the window and said, "Hope this makes you feel really good."

Angela turned this story around as if she were innocently driving down the road and Breakstone had been following her, then harassed her.

80

(Article continued with statement by Angela.) "'Mr. Breakstone seems to not remember that we are divorced,' Angela said.

"Steve Breakstone said that it was Angela Breakstone who hit him in the face on several occasions during their 14-year marriage. 'I've never raised a hand, ever,' he said.

"The past year at work has been problematic for Steve Breakstone, with three internal affairs investigations conducted into his behavior.

"Police Chief Mikel Hollaway suspended Breakstone for three days on Jan. 17 for allegations he misused police databases to find someone who wrote a bad check to an acquaintance, an internal affairs report states."

Once again, here's what really happened…

Breakstone never got suspended. Most certainly this information the journalist was getting was from Brian in Internal Affairs, who wanted to make Breakstone's life miserable. It appeared Brian was taking this opportunity to drop information to the press and while continuing his hatred towards Breakstone.

As for the allegations in the article, Breakstone received a call from a friend who owned a pawn shop. "This guy wrote us a bad check for $17,000. Is there anything you can do?"

"Well, it's a felony," Breakstone said.

"I don't want anyone getting in trouble. We do a lot of business with these people. I just need them to make this right."

Breakstone thought about the situation. It was common for a friend to call in for a favor. It wasn't anything illegal. They just wanted to avoid police reports and sending people to jail.

Breakstone said, "I'll see what I can do."

Since the person who wrote the bad check did business with the pawn shop on many occasions and this was the first bad experience, perhaps this could be worked out.

Breakstone used the police data base to locate the guy, then approached him and explained, "Look, you will be charged with a felony for the bad check. Since you've done business with the pawn shop and they actually want to continue doing business with you without any hard feelings, consider making this right."

The man agreed to do everything he could to pay them back.

In the old days, an officer would help others like this, but now, an officer cannot do this without opening an investigation. This keeps cops away from the temptation of taking a percentage of recovering the money owed. Technically, Breakstone could be prosecuted for working things out between the two businesses.

Breakstone was given a warning by his boss.

Years later, the $17,000 was paid back to the pawn shop. Included with the check was a note saying, "Please tell Steve Breakstone we're sorry for getting him in trouble."

Despite Breakstone receiving a warning for helping solve this problem without clogging up the court system, he was involved in a plan to place all pawnshop transactions in a software program, rather than officers having to sift through mounds of documents to find what they're looking for.

With a few clicks of the button, an officer could access a pawn shop customer's receipt, driver's license information, thumbprint and signature. Breakstone informed the media, "You can download 65 transactions in two seconds."

This new system became a critical tool in locating stolen goods.

Of course, this wasn't mentioned in the article made to bash Breakstone's reputation. Instead the journalist said that Breakstone, "Misused police databases to find someone who wrote a bad check to an acquaintance."

81

(The following letter was never made public or given to the media. It was written to Steve Breakstone by Lieutenant Jeff Palmer.)

I would like to take this opportunity to recommend Officer Steve Breakstone for the Distinguished Service Medal. This nomination is a result of a single action by Officer Breakstone as well as his continued actions over the last year while working in my command.

Officer Breakstone was on routine patrol when he spotted a vehicle with the rear vent window broken out. He felt this was suspicious and that this was a sign that the vehicle was possibly stolen.

He requested an additional unit to assist him and the suspect vehicle was stopped. The driver was contacted, and it was determined that he had no driver's license. The driver gave officers consent to search his vehicle.

During the search, Officer Breakstone located two $2.00 bills under a pillow that the driver had been sitting on while driving. The bills had sequential serial numbers and some red dye on them. In the glove compartment, a large quantity of small bills with red dye on them were also found.

A check with detectives revealed that the vehicle matched the description of a vehicle that was used in a bank robbery. Detectives were summoned to the scene, and it was determined that the subject was a suspect in several bank robberies.

I have since been advised that he and a partner have been linked to seven bank robberies in the area.

This incident is really typical of the type of work that Officer Breakstone performs on a regular basis. During the past year he has been involved in numerous narcotics arrests, seizing crack cocaine, marijuana, and in one instance automatic weapons from known drug dealers.

During many of the drug arrests, Officer Breakstone placed himself in harm's way, displaying courage above and beyond the call of duty. I have found his instincts to be excellent.

On one occasion, Officer Breakstone had just finished taking a burglary report where the suspect had left a shoe print on a piece of wood paneling. Officer Breakstone took the wood panel into evidence and was transporting to the police department to be processed by criminalistics. On his way to the police station, he observed a possible suspect and stopped to interview him.

During the interview, the subject was asked to show Officer Breakstone the soles of his shoes. The soles turned out to be a perfect match right down to a pebble that was embedded in the tread.

I am regularly receiving compliments about Officer Breakstone's work product. I recently received a letter from the State Attorney's Office complimenting Officer Breakstone on his testimony during a homicide trial. The letter indicated that his testimony was extremely professional and that it proved crucial in convicting the accused party.

I feel that Officer Breakstone is deserving of the Distinguished Service Medal. His performance on the job is highly professional. He displays courage on a regular basis while going out of his way to arrest street level drug dealers. He displays an everyday initiative that is uncommon in most of our police officers.

82

Twenty years ago, three teenagers in a car decided to spend their Halloween night smashing mailboxes. What the teens didn't know, was they smashed so many mailboxes that the amount became a felony.

When Breakstone caught up to the three teens, he brought them to the police station and called their parents.

Next, Breakstone called all the mailbox owners and put everyone in the same room with the teens and their parents.

"Here's the deal," Breakstone said. "The owners of the mailboxes have two choices. First, you could press felony charges. Or…" He looked at the three teenagers. "If they replace every mailbox they damaged, then I'll just write an incident report."

Right away the teens, parents, and mailbox owners agreed to have the mailboxes replaced instead of pressing charges.

Breakstone was investigated by Internal Affairs and warned not to do this again. It was dangerous because it's difficult to know if an officer was doing it just for some sort of personal gain.

Years later, "Community Policing," is common, just as Breakstone had done in that situation. In fact, doing something like this would have received him a medal.

Also the police do offer things like "Drug Court" to help drug offenders get their life back on track without getting a record.

When Breakstone visited the person who wrote the bad check, while in uniform, he encouraged him to pay to avoid criminal charges, similar to what they would have done in Community Policing or Drug Court.

And yes, twenty years ago Breakstone was investigated for offering three teenagers a choice to replace damaged mailboxes, rather than facing felony charges.

Reporters were taking bits and pieces of Breakstone's past and twisting the information to make him look like a police officer who had a career of wrong doings and suspicious behavior.

The bottom line, officers really don't want to see people get hurt. If there's a better way, most will take it.

That's all Breakstone was doing…helping people.

83

(Sarasota Herald-Tribune Article.)

In April, the state attorney's office declined to file a battery charge against Breakstone after a complaint was filed against him that he slapped the face of a jogger who confronted him about his dog's behavior.

This was another example of a journalist taking a story and only reporting a portion of the facts. Here's what really happened…

Shalom, Breakstone's youngest daughter, was seven-years-old at the time. (Yes, another case the journalist pulled up that was many years ago.) Shalom had been outside with their dog when a jogger went by the house and the dog barked at him.

The jogger stopped and yelled, "Get that dog away from me!"

Shalom petted the dog, who was now sitting by her.

The jogger then yelled, "If you don't get that dog away from me I'm going to kill it."

Shalom burst into tears.

Breakstone hurried outside. "What's the matter, honey?"

"This man is going to shoot our dog."

Breakstone walked across the lawn. "Listen, I know everyone in the neighborhood and you don't live here. Just keep going where you're going and don't say things like that to my daughter."

The jogger shoved Breakstone.

As a reaction, Breakstone slapped the guy on the side of the head. "Get off my property! Now!"

When the man wouldn't leave, Breakstone called the police and the jogger received a trespass warning.

84

(New article released…)

RULING IN FAVOR OF EX-WIFE COULD END CAREER OF 25-YEAR VETERAN LIEUTENANT

A judge granted a protective injunction against a veteran Sarasota police lieutenant Friday, a ruling that threatens to end his 25-year career on the force.

At a two-hour hearing, Lt. Steven Breakstone's ex-wife showed the judge sexual text messages he sent her and testified about how his relentless pursuit of her since their July divorce has taken on overt religious overtones and caused her fear.

It was outrageous that the journalist was using religion as a way to add more to his story. In reality, Breakstone never pressured his wife about God, especially since he had so much to learn himself.

People like this journalist seem to always bring up the same God they don't believe in. Breakstone doesn't need to pressure people about God, since God does things His own loving way.

After these lies began to show up in newspapers, Breakstone told Angela, "You're going to have to live with yourself. I never threatened you or did anything of these things."

85

(Article continued.) Angela Breakstone told the judge she even keeps a gun near her at night. "I'm afraid he'll come into my home, rape me, because I'm not responding to him," she said on the witness stand.

Of course Angela knew that Breakstone bought her that gun for protection against gang members, drug dealers, and hitmen; all of which were after him. The gun was listed on Breakstone's name, not Angela.

The article made it seem like a frightened wife walked into a gun shop, purchased a gun, then after the waiting period, brought the gun home to protect herself.

Probably the worst was the journalist claimed Breakstone was a rapist. There's no shame or responsibility in the media anymore. Breakstone's family, friends, and church members would read this and look at him differently.

86

(Article continued.) Senior Judge Nancy Donnellan found that Steven Breakstone, 47, had stalked and cyberstalked his ex-wife, even though she found no acts of physical violence and he promised the judge he would no longer bother his ex-wife.

"You have willfully harassed her, and you've been doing it for several months, despite her asking you repeatedly to stop," Donnellan told Steven Breakstone.

Breakstone, who is paid $94,794 annually as one of four shift commanders to oversee three sergeants and all patrol operations, shook his head in disbelief when he heard the ruling. "I may not be employed after this," he told the judge.

What really happened…

Breakstone never remembered saying to the judge he might not be employed after this, especially since he didn't do any of those things, or was officially working at the police department.

Breakstone did remember telling the judge, "Your decision is much more impactful to my family than just making a decision just to make a judgement." (That statement wasn't printed the newspaper.)

What Breakstone meant was that any woman can go into court based on facts or no facts, and ask for a restraining order. Then the newspapers can write about the judgement, despite Breakstone being innocent.

Here's the kicker, which wasn't mentioned in the newspaper article, yet was recorded in the court transcript. Breakstone had proved that his wife and her attorney altered the text message dates and what the messages said.

One example was a text from Breakstone saying to Angela, "Miss you too, seeing you in underwear."

Breakstone said to the judge, "Your honor, please read this message again. It's a response."

Judge: "I don't have the text message in front of me."

Breakstone: "Okay, but the message is basic language. I am responding to her by saying, 'I miss you too.' For that to happen, Angela must have originally written me a message saying that she 'missed me.'"

The judge relooked at the text messages provided by Angela and her attorney. It was discovered that all of them were falsified.

When the judge asked for an explanation, the attorney said, "It was an accident."

No perjury charges were filed against Angela or her attorney, nor was any of this mentioned in the article.

87

(Article continued.) The problem for Steven Breakstone is that the one-year injunction prohibits him from possessing a firearm, a key tool for a law enforcement officer both on and off duty. Breakstone fears Sarasota police officials may now try to fire him for conduct unbecoming an officer.

Steven Breakstone is on administrative leave pending the outcome of the stalking allegations, including an investigation by the Sarasota Sheriff's Office in which a detective who investigated has recommended criminal charges be filed against Steven Breakstone. Prosecutors will ultimately decide if charges are warranted.

The sheriff's investigator wrote in a memo to the State Attorney's Office about Steven Breakstone's "escalating bizarre behavior" since his divorce.

Steven Breakstone is also currently appealing a three-day suspension in another internal affairs case.

—

Breakstone was never suspended for any of this, nor were any charges filed. The reason was simple…

He never did any of these things and there was nothing to suspend him from.

Breakstone asked the journalist to print a retraction, but the journalist claimed he couldn't do that.

88

Back in 1996, there had been a white male approaching grocery stores with a note saying, "Give me the money!"

There weren't any reports of the robber having a gun, yet, the cashiers didn't take that chance; they just gave him the money.

Breakstone and the other officers were now on the lookout for this guy. His description was the same with each grocery employee: White male, thinning blonde hair, wearing a red and black jogging suit.

One evening Breakstone was in the passenger seat while Detective Bob Gorvan was driving. They passed the Ford dealership and Breakstone noticed a man walking down the street wearing a red and black jogging suit. Besides the suit, he also fit the description.

"That's the guy!" Breakstone said to Detective Gorvan. "Pull over!"

Gorvan swerved the car to the side and they jumped out, quickly approaching the man.

Breakstone couldn't believe his eyes. He knew the man!

Terry McKenna worked as a bouncer for Animal House and had plenty of contact with Breakstone over the years.

McKenna softened his gaze. "It's over…isn't it?"

Breakstone placed his hand on McKenna's shoulder. "It's over if you want it to be."

They arrested McKenna and took him to the Detective Bureau. McKenna confessed to all of the robberies.

Breakstone asked, "Why were you robbing these places? Are you having money troubles?"

A tear drizzled from McKenna's eye. "Crack…I'm over the top with it." He paused, avoiding eye contact. "I just want a better life. I want to be a better person."

Breakstone stood and shut off the interview tape. He thought about Joe and how easy it was to drift away. If Joe was here, he would tell McKenna the same thing Breakstone was about to say.

"Listen, Terry, the only way you can be a better person is with God. It's obviously not going to happen on your own."

Tears drained down McKenna's face. "I'm going prison. My life is over."

Breakstone guided McKenna from the chair and they both kneeled in the interview room. Breakstone closed his eyes and prayed for McKenna, asking Jesus to save him.

When he finished, they both stood. Breakstone locked his eyes on McKenna and said, "Terry, you're going to prison. There's no way around it. But that doesn't have to be the end of your journey to God. It's just a season. You'll get through it."

McKenna pled guilty and received five years. Breakstone sent stamps to McKenna along with some money so McKenna could send people letters who he cared about and wanted to ask forgiveness.

A few years later, Breakstone received a letter from McKenna. He had been placed in a halfway house. About a year later, he was free, got married and started a family.

McKenna attended church regularly and volunteered for youth football. Breakstone got him a job as an equipment manager, because McKenna was having trouble finding work. He fixed helmets and pads, which gave him a purpose to continue moving forward.

Unfortunately McKenna's humbling season returned years later. He was in a car accident and given prescription drugs to help with the pain and his recovery.

However, the opposite happened. The prescription drugs became a gateway for McKenna to fall back into his drug habit. He lost his job, his wife, family, and was once again at rock bottom.

Breakstone received a letter from a halfway house in Arkansas. It was short, with these words, "Brother, can you help me? I need you to pray for me…Terry McKenna."

Over the years, Breakstone continued praying for McKenna with the memory of Joe attached to those prayers and the notion that anyone can get off the ugly streets by entering the doors of church.

"The steps of a good man are ordered by the Lord, and He delights in his way. Though he fall, he shall not be utterly cast down; For the Lord upholds him with His hand." ~ Psalm 94:18-19

89

(Article in, Behind the Blue Wall.)

This article had a photo of a silhouette man walking in a room. It was something you'd see in a serial killer movie. The writer of the article said, "I opted to not post the photo of Steve Breakstone that I found. This is potentially lethal and I'm praying."

Breakstone read the words over again.

Potentially lethal.

I'm praying.

So the writer of this article didn't want to post a picture of Breakstone, because he was terrified Breakstone would come after the guy. This made zero sense.

Basically, the writer wanted to add a silhouette picture and say words like "lethal" to increase the amount of readers.

In the opening headline of the article it said, "Police Officer Involved Domestic Violence."

Then the article began…

"We are lighting a candle of remembrance for those who've lost their lives to domestic violence behind the Blue Wall, for strength and wisdom to those still there, and a non-ending prayer for those who thought they had escaped, but can't stop being afraid."

Breakstone's mouth about hit the floor. Now a group was lighting a candle over something Breakstone never did. He could envision the group gathered in a park at night, holding up their candles, praying to stop domestic violence from police officers.

This wouldn't be wrong, except they were doing this because of him!

The rest of the article was a replay of what was already written by someone else, with a few different twists.

Breakstone read this new version…

90

INJUNCTION FILED AGAINST SARASOTA POLICE OFFICER ACCUSED OF STALKING

Sarasota police Lt. Steven Breakstone testifies in court Friday in Sarasota. A judge granted a protective injunction against Breakstone; his ex-wife accuses him of stalking her.

Breakstone stopped reading for a moment. What was the point? It was more of the same. He wanted to dig out his large blue folder of awards and commendations, go to the office of the tribune and find the writer of the Blue Wall and toss the folder on their desk.

Would it do any good? Probably not.

As for this article, Breakstone couldn't help himself. He skimmed over it, noticing some different things written about him.

(Article continued.) Steven Breakstone said he would "live a quiet life" and leave her alone.

But the lieutenant remained emphatic his ex-wife lied in the courtroom about the nature of their contact, specifically that she was not always telling her to leave him alone.

Angela Breakstone — who moved only three houses away after the split — admitted to having sex with her ex-husband since the divorce. Steven Breakstone says it happened twice.

And several of the racy text messages sent by Breakstone appear to be responses to text messages from his wife.

"I thought there was still a part of her that cared," Breakstone said after the hearing.

This is her second petition for protection; she said the first one in December 2010 was not granted because Steven Breakstone has been friends with the judge for more than 20 years. This time, two judges who were former prosecutors have recused themselves from hearing the case.

Angela Breakstone's petition claims he harassed her in traffic, went into her house without her permission, appears unannounced at her home, brought her plates of food and baked her cookies.

The petition requires Steven Breakstone to stay 200 feet from her home and 50 feet from her employer. The custody and visitation schedule for their three children remains the same.

What the article did not state was that a few years before this, Breakstone was given an award, "In Recognition of a Career Achievement, Successful Performance in the Civil Service Examination Process, Dedication to Duty and for his Committed Service to the Citizens of Sarasota." He was then promoted to Lieutenant.

This was certainly a contradiction of what's being printed in the media.

91

Breakstone shook his head. On the right side of this article were links to past articles by the writer. They included:

"Corrections Officer in Washington: Arrested for terroristic threats and domestic violence assault charges." Next to the headline was a pic of prison bars.

Breakstone read the next link. "NOPD Officer Lacour convicted of shooting gun outside ex's house." There was a cheap photo shop pic of a marshal badge. Obviously not much thought was put into it.

In fact, no thought was put into any of this! It was like they took past media bashing of officers and threw gasoline on the fire so it would shine brighter than ever.

Breakstone had gone to court and won. This cleared his name and proved what his ex-wife had been doing. During the testimonies, all the truth came out, which included Breakstone and his wife were having consensual sex, the text messages were consensual, the gun was registered in his name to help protect her because there was a contract out on Breakstone's life, and most of all, everything stated in the media was complete and utter fabrication.

Before all of this started, Breakstone had felt bad about the breakup and all the things he had done wrong. He was going to give his ex-wife a check for $100,000, rather than her fight for half of his retirement and other funds.

No one reported this, because the media could sell more papers by bashing a police officer without justification.

Breakstone once again approached the reporter who led the attack and asked that he rewrite the truth. Of course, the reporter refused.

Since no one would print a retraction, the other media outlets continued to destroy Breakstone by writing what would sell the best.

92

(Articles continued to appear about Breakstone. Here are the highlights…)

"A longtime Sarasota Police lieutenant stalking his ex-wife." (Not true.)

"Entering her home when she was not there." (Not true, except for the one time when he made sure there wasn't a burglar.)

"Sending her numerous explicit text messages." (Twisted truth.)

"Escalating bizarre behavior since his divorce became final." (Not true. In fact, Breakstone felt horrible about what happened and wanted to find forgiveness with God.)

"The Sarasota Police Department put Breakstone on administrative leave." (Not True. He was retired.)

"Breakstone has had several contentious disciplinary battles in his 25-year career at the department." (Not true. Breakstone was made officer of the year and rose to his status faster than anyone else in history of Sarasota Police Department.)

"This is her second petition for protection; she said the first one in December 2010 was not granted because Steve Breakstone has been friends with the judge for more than 20 years." (Did the newspaper really think a judge would toss a case out based on friendship? Such an accusation should have brought a huge legal action on the newspaper.)

"Steve Breakstone told sheriff's investigators he has strong religious beliefs that are guiding him to try to reunite with his ex-wife." (Strong religious beliefs were made to sound like Breakstone was using the church as an excuse to become a stalker. Once again, absolutely not true!)

"The past year at work has been problematic for Steve Breakstone, with three internal affairs investigations conducted into his behavior." (Not true!)

Not true!

Not true!

Breakstone couldn't take the lies anymore. He just wanted to move on with his life, but the world was intending on destroying him to the point there was nothing left.

"'You will not certainly die,' the serpent said to the woman." ~ Genesis 3:4 By the way, that was a lie as well.)

93

There was a link to one of the articles about Breakstone, connected to a website called, Police Prostitution and Politics: Commercial Sex Scandals in America.

Breakstone was mixed in with officers who were charged with domestic violence, along with officers involved with murder/suicides.

As the year went on, the media bashing continued. Breakstone was even thrown into an article for an arrest when he wasn't even there!

The title of article from the YouObserver.com was, "SPD (Sarasota Police Department) Wrong to Arrest Homeless Man for Charging Phone."

The first line in the article was, "I wasn't planning on doing any writing today, but I could only shake my head in disbelief when I visited the Sarasota Herald-Tribune website and read the cover story about a homeless man being arrested for 'stealing utilities' Sunday night because he was charging his cell phone at an electrical outlet in the Gillespie Park gazebo."

This enraged Breakstone. Once again someone took an article from somewhere else, twisted it, then posted his version in the Arts & Entertainment section of the website.

Let's repeat that…Arts & Entertainment.

The writer felt it was important to bash police officers in a section made for theatre, ballet performances and stories about local artists.

After a long rant of how the homeless person was wronged by police, the writer didn't stop there. He began a bashing on new Police Chief, Mike

Halloway and how he should be, "Embarrassed by his officer's performance."

What did this all have to do with Breakstone? Nothing. However, the writer found a way to twist a knife into Breakstone as well.

The article went on, "Kersey's arrest follows on the heels of SPD officer Sam Patrick being fired for repeatedly punching a suspect in the head while making an arrest near the Ivory Lounge in downtown Sarasota. In January, Lt. Steve Breakstone had an injunction filed against him for stalking and harassing his ex-wife.

"And who can forget the 2009 Juan Perez case in which officer Christopher Childers was captured on video kicking a handcuffed and intoxicated prisoner after he climbed out the back window of Childers' squad car while Childers sat in the front seat of the parked car working on his in-car computer.

"The Childers incident cost Childers and former Police Chief Peter Abbott their jobs in 2010, but was anybody really surprised when the city's sham of a citizen review panel gave Childers his job back in September – with more than two years of back pay thrown in for good measure?

"Are these the kind of officers we want protecting and serving our city? I don't think so."

Was the writer finished? Not by a long shot. He continued on and on, bashing police officers.

And yes, this was considered, Arts & Entertainment…

94

Another article discussed everything about the Sarasota Police Department, then added a few words about how Breakstone was being investigated for, "escalating bizarre behavior." By the way, other links near the article led viewers to pictures of women who had shown their privates during weddings, sports, and events. Real classy writing.

Even on Wikipedia for Sarasota Police Department, Breakstone is mentioned in the section under, "Misconduct" with officers who have been accused of crimes. "Police Lieutenant Steven Breakstone was put on administrative leave to allow an investigation."

Could Wikipedia print false information? Apparently they could, which begs to question, "What can you trust about Wikipedia?"

As Breakstone read article after article, it appeared everyone used the same words, "Escalating bizarre behavior." To this day, Breakstone had no idea what that meant, nor did he conduct himself that way, but one paper printed the story and everyone jumped on.

Note: Not printed in the article were Breakstone's awards. Just some of them included:

- *Expert Infantry Badge*
- *Distinguished Service Medal*
- *Army Good Conduct Medal*
- *Three times awarded Meritorious Service Medal*
- *Two Unit Commendations*
- *Humanitarian Service Award*
- *Police Officer of the Year*

"The insults that are hurled at you have fallen on Me." ~ Romans 15:3

95

The crazy thing is Breakstone could have fed the media enough heroic stories of the Sarasota Police Department to cover years of articles. Despite this, they just wanted to write about corruption, hate, and stories that would tear down good people.

Breakstone had over 1,000 arrests in his career and had a year with over 160 felony arrests, along with very high prosecution rates. This is great for society and keeping the streets safe, but not great for people who get jealous.

There was a time when Breakstone received a call for a homicide. A white male was stabbed in the neck, hit an artery, and died just seconds later.

As Breakstone arrived on the scene to find the dead body, a typical Florida rainstorm came down so hard, he couldn't see two feet in front of him. Also, any evidence was now being destroyed.

About a block away was a place nicknamed, House of Pain. Breakstone knew the place well, since it was a crack house run by two brothers.

With the evidence being washed away in the rain, Breakstone figured this would be a good place to start, especially since it was close the crime scene.

There was an overhang over the front door. As Breakstone approached, he noticed blood in the doorframe. Breakstone envisioned the victim stumbling from the house with blood sprouting from his neck. But since the knife wound was in his neck, there was no way he could have made it a few blocks away.

Breakstone knocked on door, then entered.

Angela Willis was inside. She was a prostitute that Breakstone repeatedly said, "God has a plan for you."

There were a couple other prostitutes in the house as well, all on the floor, wrapped in blankets.

Breakstone approached Angela. "Is there anything you want to tell me?"

Angela tightened the blanket around her shoulders. "Man, Stone…things are messed up." She then shifted her eyes to the other side of the room, where a man named Johnny Kneely was standing in the corner. He had bright red hair, pale skin, and his body was like a thin pole.

Breakstone leaned forward and whispered in Angela's ear, "God has a plan for you. I'm going to keep saying that until you believe it."

He then approached Kneely and asked if he'd come to the police station for questioning.

96

Interview Room

Breakstone read Kneely his Myranda Rights. He asked, "Do you want to tell me what happened?"

Kneely: "I'd rather not."

Breakstone knew that most interrogators would hammer away more questions. However, he had a different approach.

Breakstone re-read Kneely's Myranda Rights and said, "I just want to make it crystal clear that you don't have to speak with me if you do not wish."

This was risk, because he was basically giving Kneely a way out. They didn't have any evidence, since it washed away in the rain. There was blood on the door, but there were ten people inside the crack house. Breakstone was certain Kneely was his guy, but he had to prove it beyond a reasonable doubt.

Suddenly Kneely cleared his throat and began rocking back and forth. "I didn't know the guy who got killed."

Breakstone: "I just want the truth. By you claiming not to know the victim, then I believe you're not being honest with me."

Kneely continued rocking back and forth. "Okay, I got into a fight with the dude."

Breakstone: "What about?"

Kneely: "The cracker wouldn't shut up!"

Breakstone: "How did you feel?" He paused, leaning closer. "Come on, tell me how you felt about him not shutting up."

Kneeling squeezed his fist and subconsciously made a stabbing motion. "I told him to shut up! He wouldn't stop!"

Breakstone: "I know, you said that. How did it make you feel?"

Kneely raised his closed fist and yelled, "I stabbed him! That's right, I stabbed him! If I had a brick next to me, I would have smashed his skull!"

Breakstone remained calm. "How did the victim get from the house to a location a few blocks away?"

Kneely: "I saw two dudes pick him up, put him in the back of their truck, and drive away."

Breakstone then arrested Kneely for murder.

97

State Attorney Earl Moreland claimed that if Detective Breakstone had treated this like most interrogating officers, "We would have lost the case."

During trial, Breakstone was asked to testify. The defense filed three motions to suppress testimonies, but lost them all because of the way Breakstone handled the case, especially since he did not violate the defendant's Constitutional Rights.

Kneely was sentenced to life in prison.

State Attorney Earl Moreland: "Justice prevailed in this case largely due to the efforts of Detective Breakstone and all the other members of the Sarasota Police Department who were involved in this investigation."

Breakstone thought about the stabbing case. It was all over one guy being annoying. Someone died and other one sent to prison over talking too much.

There had been another case when a husband and wife were arguing. She grabbed a paring knife and stabbed him in the chest.

When Breakstone arrived on the scene, he kneeled down and realized the man was going to die; blood was pouring from his chest.

Breakstone leaned close and said to the man, "If you have something to tell me, do it now, because you're going to die."

The man coughed up blood and said, "I took the last can of beer."

He died a few seconds later.

Normally someone could be saved from a chest stabbing, but the wife just happened to shove the paring knife in the one spot that would kill him in minutes.

This was all over a can of beer.

What happened behind the scenes with the Kneely case and other horrifying cases is mostly withheld from the media. It's not like on television where detectives are heroes to the public. In reality, most of the information remains as internal victories, like the comments from State Attorney Earl Moreland. His quote wasn't printed in the newspaper article.

Instead, it was given to Breakstone and his chief via a private letter.

98

Years later, the Florida Department of Law Enforcement Quarterly Update decided to give Breakstone one last reminder that his past, which was blurred by speculation and lies, will continue to haunt. They mentioned misconduct, stalking, giving false statements, and perjury.

Breakstone suddenly discovered why Angela made those false statements to his chief and to the press.

Breakstone and Angela's incomes were equal at the time of their divorce, so the court did not order child support. When Angela spoke to her friends, they told her she should set him up for things he didn't do, make him look bad, get the kids, and then she'll be able to earn the right to child support.

Friends shouldn't encourage harm, retaliation, or making a problem worse, but that's exactly what they did with Angela. What they didn't consider is what all of this would do to Angela and the kids. All they had on the brain was destroying Breakstone because the marriage didn't work out for the best.

Also, Angela's friends didn't consider how difficult it would be to setup an innocent person for something they never did, nor did they consider it ever backfiring on Angela.

When the day came for Angela to come clean, Breakstone knew her friends would hide in the shadows, letting Angela deal with it on her own.

If all this wasn't enough, her friends most certainly loved the false media stories about Breakstone, but never considered the damage being done to the Sarasota Police Department. If any of Angela's friends needed a police officer, would they apologize for the bad press?

Probably not.

Breakstone had been an expert witness for street level narcotics, won awards based on his courtroom testimonies, and never been suspended or committed perjury.

Despite that, if you get a few people together and start rumors, nothing else seems to matter.

"Let no corrupting talk come out of your mouths, but only such as is good for building up, that it may give grace to those who hear." ~ Ephesians 4:29

99

Breakstone made a pledge to completely boycott the news and urged others to do the same. He committed himself to avoiding a simple click on an Internet story, which he now calls, "Ridiculous propaganda machines."

There was a day when reporters like Walter Cronkite would report the news and not editorialize it. After all, it was Cronkite's coverage of the 1952 Republican and Democratic National Conventions that brought to life the phrase "news anchor." He was the example of responsible reporting.

It's difficult to learn the facts these days when watching the news without considering whose reporting and what agenda they have. (Especially when it comes to money.)

As for Breakstone, he's doesn't want anything to do with the dribble they claim is news. He never to read another article in the newspaper, listen to news radio, or watch news on the television.

How could he? There was a good chance that just about every story was fueled with lies and embellishment to earn a profit.

Ignoring the media while gaining his wisdom only from the Holy Spirit seemed like a better choice. His life became less stressful and the hatred towards others was replaced by love.

"We do not speak in words taught by human wisdom, but in words taught by the Spirit." ~ 1 Corinthians 2:13

100

Despite being on his own; no family, no career, Breakstone's bulletproof feeling had crept back.

How could this be after everything he learned? Well, it just slithered into his life like a snake slithers through the grass.

Perhaps the media wore him down. Breakstone didn't want to believe anything or anyone could hurt him. If Breakstone was really honest with himself, then he could admit that he still didn't have a firm relationship with God.

The bulletproof theory might help get over his divorce, or not seeing his kids as much, and not having the passion of protecting others as a police officer, but would it help Breakstone with his relationship to God?

All his life, Breakstone was going through the motions. Whenever there had been problems in his marriage, Breakstone didn't use love as a solution, or turn upward to God. Instead, he used his bulletproof mentally and tried to fix things his way.

He felt there was always a way he could repair and find a way through, which led him into a darker place, rather than becoming closer to his wife and closer to children.

Most importantly, it prevented himself from having a close relationship with God. In fact, Breakstone continued to drift farther away.

Breakstone had prayed to be loved. God sent a friend to prove that love does exist, especially from God. Apparently that Myracle wasn't enough, although, it should have been.

God gave Breakstone the bible and church to show he is loved, but that wasn't enough. God helped Breakstone bring Joe to church, but that wasn't enough to soften Breakstone's heart.

Instead, Breakstone replaced his with his "tough guy" attitude. This was no better than Joe on the streets selling drugs. Both of them had actually felt more comfortable in the darkness. If they didn't, then it wouldn't be so easy to return.

Breakstone continued using women by meeting for coffee; drawn in by their overwhelming kindness. There was a right path to love, but Breakstone took the path to destruction. Instead of finding love, he destroyed the women he had affairs with, destroyed his wife, and destroyed the loving principles he learned when attending church.

Not only that, Breakstone destroyed the teachings in the bible which he dedicated himself to read. He destroyed the small groups that prayed for him. He destroyed the songs in church and the volunteering he had done. None of it mattered if he wasn't going down the path chosen for him by God.

Still, Breakstone kept telling himself that he was bulletproof. It was the only way to not feel guilty about what he'd been doing.

The amazing thing was Breakstone had no problem battling with Joe to get him to church and on the right path. Breakstone never gave up until Joe's soul had been saved.

Why couldn't he do that for himself?

Breakstone told prostitutes, "God has a plan for you." He repeated that phrase every time he saw them. Yet, was Breakstone actually trying to convince himself of that notion?

101

In the middle of the night, Breakstone was alone, lying in bed, wide awake. He gazed in the darkness at the ceiling, unable to produce a single comforting thought that would calm his nerves.

Suddenly Breakstone felt like someone was right in his face, nose-to-nose. His heart banged against his chest. He couldn't move.

It was the presence of God. (Yes, God was getting in his face.)

Two words were then spoken to him, "You're done."

Breakstone still couldn't move. His mind went off in a thousand directions.

You're done.

Those two words had countless meanings.

You're done with doing things your own way.

You're done heading in your own direction.

You're done leading your life.

You're done.

God needed Breakstone to surrender. There wasn't a second option, or some other choice.

You're done.

Then God spoke one more word like a bullhorn in Breakstone's ears, "Surrender."

It was a word that pounded into his soul. Surrendering was the only thing Breakstone would never do. In fact, it was the only thing he didn't know how to do.

Surrender? No way!

It meant he would have to give up. Surrender meant failure. It meant he's not accomplished enough to do the things that had to be done.

Worst of all, it meant he was weak.

God used the Holy Spirit to show Breakstone that his thinking must be completely changed. Surrender didn't mean he was in the worst place ever; it meant he was in the best place he could be. Surrender meant he would be walking side-by-side with God.

"Get comfortable being uncomfortable. This is how you break the plateau and reach the next level." ~ Chalene Johnson

102

There's a destiny placed in all of our hearts, which can be seen in the far distance. Like most people, Breakstone had only seen one path to his destiny, but God in His infinite wisdom would take him along several difficult paths to break him down and build him back up again.

Breakstone had been trying to take the path of least resistance. By doing this, it would sacrifice experience, knowledge, and the opportunity to become spiritually stronger.

On other hand, if God showed Breakstone the entire path, he probably would have turned on his heels because it was too difficult and even too humiliating.

When God brought Joe into church, he was given just a glimpse. If God had broken Joe down when he was younger and clearly showed the path he would have to take in order to reach heaven, Joe would have been so far away and would've never taken one step near the church.

Traveling in the valley of death, Breakstone, Joe, and all others are much closer to God. Those humbling experiences become beautiful ways to mature as a Christian.

In Exodus 17:12, Aaron and Hur hold Moses's arms up when he became tired. This is what God does for us through a variety of ways. We have Christian brothers and sisters who will hold our arms up until we regain the strength needed to move forward. That's when the beauty of Christ can been seen.

Breakstone held Joe's arm up until Joe stood on his own in church and courageously spoke what was on his heart.

Behind the scenes, there was a men's group holding Breakstone's arm up and Linford Sommers holding the other arm up, pressing his hands toward heaven and turning his life over to the powerful name of Jesus.

103

When Breakstone became engaged a third time, the woman ended up calling him and said, "I'm going to send the ring back."

At this point, Breakstone would usually fall to pieces. His weakness of not wanting to be alone would rip him apart if he didn't get some control over this feeling.

So instead of falling to pieces, Breakstone fell on his knees in prayer and opened the Word of God. The Holy Spirit said, "You're not on the bulletproof path anymore. You're on God's path. It's not about Steve Breakstone. It's about surrendering your life to God and understanding the true beauty of succeeding on higher levels while helping others do the same."

When God tore him down, Breakstone responded by saying, "I'm shredded to the core and of no value to you now."

God responded by saying, "It's the opposite. Now I can finally use you, because Steve Breakstone is out of the way."

"We struggle and work hard because we have placed our hope in the living God, who is the savior of all and especially of those who believe." ~ 1 Timothy 4:10

104

In San Francisco, California, Breakstone attended a personal development training course called, PSI, which has worked with hundreds of thousands of people all over the world, helping them discover their ultimate effectiveness through breakthrough educational programs.

In the middle of the night on the ranch, once again he felt God's presence. Like Moses, Breakstone made his way up a hill and stood in the darkness, waiting for the Holy Spirit to speak.

Moments later, Breakstone was given an image of children playing and him coaching football.

During the training, they had been taught on how to recognize negative things in life along with positive things. God was saying to Breakstone, "Look over this hill and see all the wonderful things that life has to offer you and others."

Breakstone took a moment, gazing into the darkness, attempting to see as far as possible over the hill. He spoke with a whisper, "But God, surly there will be negative things to hold me back."

God responded, "Who do you belong to?"

Breakstone had another image. "I belong to Your Son, Jesus Christ."

After meditating throughout the night, Breakstone walked back down the hill, seeing clearly what his mission in life had become.

105

Breakstone wasn't the only one who received an image that evening. He got a call from his good friend, Linford Sommers, who was the same person that brought Breakstone the letter of love, written by God.

This is what Linford said, "I envisioned a black and yellow snake that wrapped around you, tugging you. Jesus appeared and held his hand up and the snake was gone. Jesus then said, 'I don't want you to rewind or playback your past ever again. You don't have to apologize for what you've done…you're forgiven.' Jesus turned and pointed to a massive rusty steel sign that said, 'You're Forgiven.' Jesus said, 'Steve, you see your forgiveness like this, but I see your forgiveness like this…' Jesus touched the rusty steel sign and it turned to solid gold."

When Breakstone hung up the phone, he thought about the many highs and lows in life, but Jesus only sees the gold. No one has to earn forgiveness. If fact, it's impossible to earn and it can't be undone. It's a gift from Jesus. This is what love is all about.

"People who are proud will soon be disgraced. It is wiser to be modest." - Proverbs 11:2

It took many years for Breakstone to understand the simple fact of being humble, rather than the delusional feeling of being bulletproof. God humbled Breakstone so it was possible to strengthen him with real armor that could not be penetrated.

"Build up your strength in union with the Lord and by means of his mighty power. Put on all the armor that God gives you, so that you will be able to stand up against the Devil's evil tricks." - Ephesians 6:10-11

Breakstone discovered that his strength was terrific to justify the wrongs in his life and a great way to combat the haters. However, was it real? Or was it a house built on sand?

God's strength is deep inside and a gift that doesn't have to be bragged about, or even discussed, but rather shared as a servant of Jesus.

"The Lord says, 'Wise men should not boast of their wisdom, nor strong men of their strength, nor rich men of their wealth.'" - Jeremiah 9:23

Breakstone's glory isn't the bulletproof police officer, no more than Joe was a bulletproof leader in the streets. This is delusional protection.

The only true glory is in Christ Jesus and the only way to reach His glory is to surrender.

It's something terribly difficult for the Breakstone's and Joe's of the world, which is ironic because there was a time when they were on opposite sides of the law. It was also amazing to think that Breakstone was still lost in finding God's true purpose, but Joe became close to Jesus in a short time and surrendered in the church, then eventually surrendered in death.

When thinking about the word surrender, it became a beautiful experience in which Breakstone and Joe would forever share together.

106

The song Glorious Ruins by Hillsong talks about how you can deal with the ruins in life with the beauty of the Lord, rising up from the ashes as God reigns over all of your problems, worries, and weaknesses.

Breakstone knew that by surrendering to Jesus, he'll never be left behind. There's a simple reason for this...

Jesus isn't capable of leaving his children behind.

Breakstone could easily be fooled by Satan's smoke and mirrors, turning Breakstone's life into trash along with the lives around him. But on his knees, ignoring Satan and humbling himself before God, Breakstone can be saved from the one true enemy that was holding him back...

Breakstone.

"I can do all things through Christ who strengthens me." ~ Phillipians 4:13

107

Breakstone took a four week course in his church to develop a growth track, giving him wisdom and guidance for what God had planned for him. During the end of the growth track, Breakstone began seeing visions of poor children and families. As the ideas became stronger, he sensed these people weren't from the United States.

Then God gave Breakstone a clear vision. God wanted Breakstone to build a church in Colombia for a poor and desperate community. The church would be built in the middle as the central location for the people, along with a clinic to the right of the church.

Breakstone wanted it to be a gift to this Colombia community. When it's finished, he would leave and begin the next project that God would place in his heart.

By doing this, it would also encourage Breakstone to mature as a Christian and become stronger in his faith.

On this, Titus 1:7-9 explains the importance of planting a church and being a church leader. "For since a church leader is in charge of God's work, he should be without fault. He must not be arrogant or quick-tempered, or a drunkard or violent or greedy for money.

"He must be hospitable and love what is good. He must be self-controlled, upright, holy, and disciplined. He must hold firmly to the message which can be trusted and which agrees with the doctrine. In this way he will be able to encourage others with the true teaching and also to show the error of those who are opposed to it."

Of course, Breakstone felt he had a long way to go, but as the goal of planting a church in Colombia grew each day, so would his faith in doing the work of God.

Breakstone visited Colombia and met a woman who sold peanuts. The woman was so pleased with her job and had a beautiful smile on her face. Jesus was already in the Colombian communities; you could see it beyond the suffering of massacres, violence, and the challenges of getting through a day.

Breakstone knew in his heart that a church would, "Encourage others with the true teaching and also show the error of those who are opposed to it."

108

God has given Breakstone and all of us an open opportunity for today. What are you going to do with that opportunity? Who do you want to become?

Life is:

BE

DO

HAVE

When you realize this, you are empowered. How you are BEING? What you are DOING? This will determine what you HAVE?

Breakstone now understood this kind of thinking would allow him to help others DO the same.

"The only person you are destined to become is the person you decide to be." ~ Ralph Waldo Emerson

109

When Breakstone attended a Tony Robbins event, he had the most incredible weekend. Breakstone walked barefoot on 2000 degree burning hot coals barefoot and did not get burned.

More importantly, even with all the personal development training he had, Breakstone discovered new ways to take a step further…there's always room for improvement. There's still ways to become a better man, a better father, a better friend, and a better Christian.

During his time there, Breakstone's son Gabriel totaled his car in a wreck. Before becoming the angry father, Breakstone praised God that Gabe and the other driver were okay.

Yes, it's difficult to receive bad news. Breakstone had just learned at the Tony Robbins event to take a quick ninety seconds, think about how he feels, and respond in a way to have the greatest outcome.

"He is not afraid of receiving bad news; his faith is strong and he trusts in the Lord." - Psalms 112:7

Instead of getting angry, which was what Breakstone would have done in the past, he responded in a way to allow Gabe an opportunity to think and reflect on what happened. In the future, this may let Gabe use alternative behavior on his part, which may save his or someone else's life in the future.

Certainly people may look at Tony Robbins as a bunch of hype or bull, however, Breakstone had become passionate about improving his life, along with the lives of others. It started with his children and would spread to as many people as Breakstone could reach.

With all the love Breakstone began to feel, it had become important for people to see the world in a way that empowers them; to shape their destiny.

Despite Breakstone's passion for helping others, there are moments that are out of his control. His faith was about to be tested like never before.

110

Breakstone's son, Gabe, was an incredible laughing kind of kid. As the middle son, he did his own thing like boating and scuba diving. In fact, Gabe loved the ocean.

The really bad habit Gabe had was wrecking cars since he received his license. For some reason, he never learned his lesson. Breakstone had no choice but to sell Gabe's truck until he learned the value of owning a vehicle and also how important it was to be safe on the road. Gabe had to understand it wasn't just his safety, but the passengers and other people on the road.

On the night of August 9th, 2016, Breakstone had this weird feeling when Gabe and his sister, Shalom, asked to borrow Breakstone's truck. Gabe wanted to go out and Shalom wanted a ride to her friend's house. Breakstone was supposed to fly to Colombia the next morning and wouldn't need the truck, but there was something not right.

Despite Breakstone telling both Gabe and Shalom it wasn't a good idea, they persisted. Breakstone saw how much they wanted to use the truck and it was difficult to say no when your children ask for something, but Breakstone actually begged both Gabe and Shalom not to go.

Well, they went anyway. Shalom wrote a note saying, "Don't be mad. We love you."

Breakstone read the note several times.

Something was terribly wrong, but he didn't know what it was, or how to explain it.

111

Gabe was supposed to be home at midnight. Breakstone woke at six in the morning, walked to Gabe's bedroom, but he wasn't there.

Breakstone then looked on the driveway and didn't see his truck.

Next, he checked his phone for messages, but there wasn't any.

Of course Breakstone's mind began to wander. Maybe Gabe fell asleep somewhere. He could be at his mom's, or maybe his girlfriend's house.

Suddenly Breakstone's phone rang. He quickly answered it. "Hello?"

The caller was an old friend from the police department. She said, "I just want to say how sorry I am about what happened."

Breakstone gripped the cellphone. "Sorry about what? I don't know what you're talking about."

There was a pause. "You didn't hear what happened to Gabe?"

A drizzle of sweat ran down Breakstone's face. "No. Where is he?"

"I'll call you back." She hung up.

Breakstone quickly dressed. His mind wandered to a thousand places, wondering what happened with Gabe.

Arrested?

Wrecked his truck again?

Breakstone sat on the bed, waiting for the officer to call him back. He didn't move.

He just sat there.

Waiting.

112

The doorbell rang.

Breakstone quickly answered it, seeing it was his good friend, Corey Moody.

"What are you doing here?" Breakstone was absolutely confused.

Corey placed his hand on Breakstone's arm. "Come with me."

Breakstone entered Corey's car and he drove through the neighborhood, just a few blocks down the road. There were several cruisers with flashing lights, along with an ambulance.

When Breakstone exited the car, he saw his truck smashed into a tree. The good news was the accident didn't look horrible. There was only a minimum amount of damage.

Breakstone took a step forward, but Corey held him back. "Don't go over there."

Breakstone looked at him. "Why?"

Corey took in a deep breath. "Your son died in this accident."

Breakstone looked at the truck against the tree. "There's not enough damage to kill someone." He looked back at Corey. "How…"

Corey lowered his head. "Your son…shot himself in the head."

Breakstone felt the world slip away. He leaned against the car, eyes shifting in every direction. "Shot himself? Why?" His voice was distant.

It didn't make sense. Why would Gabe kill himself?

Did he wreck the car and feel guilty? Did he panic? Was Breakstone too hard on him? Maybe not hard enough?

He looked at the truck, envisioning the guns under the seat. They kept those for protection. Gabe knew how to clean a gun, load it and shoot it.

Gabe knew exactly what the gun was supposed to be used for…protection.

For some reason, Gabe felt the only security remaining in his life was to end it.

Breakstone called Gabe's mother and a few other friends. It was the toughest phone calls he ever had to make.

113

"And God will wipe away every tear from their eyes; there shall be no more death, nor sorrow, nor crying. There shall be no more pain, for the former things have passed away." ~ Isaiah 43:1-3

A memorial service was held four days later at the Light of the World International Church. A candlelight/lantern vigil was held a day before at Siesta Key Beach, near the yellow lifeguard stand, celebrating Gabe's life and his love for the ocean.

One of his favorite songs was, One Man Can Change the World, by Big Sean, featuring Kanye West and John Legend.

Breakstone listened to the song over and over again, letting the lyrics sink deep into his soul.

If he could love himself, just as God loved him, then he could make it through Gabe's death, then go beyond by changing the world for the better.

Everything Breakstone chose to do, every decision he made had to be real, with a sense of true purpose. Most of all, he had to remember this…

One man can change the world.

"Blessed are the pure in heart, for they shall see God." ~ Mathew 5:8

114

When Gabe was supposed to graduate high school, it brought back memories of the difficult time Gabe had as a teenager. Gabe was such a kind person and avoided the typical high school fights.

However, there was this one time when a kid touched his girlfriend inappropriately. Gabe lost his temper on the kid and a fight ensued. Gabe was suspended over this first offence.

Breakstone understood Gabe's frustrations. It didn't matter if it's a police station or a high school; local newspaper or a high school newsletter; people were going to judge and those who were innocent would from time to time, suffer from that judgment.

Breakstone did plead with the principal to remove the suspension, but he might as well have been pleading with an irate Internal Affairs officer who had a personal grudge.

When the high school held his graduation, friends and family of Gabe suggested they keep his seat open as a remembrance of Gabe.

However, the school refused.

Breakstone didn't understand. It was just one seat. The school wasn't condoning Gabe's suicide, nor would they have to make much effort to leave a seat open. Should Breakstone hold his tongue and just accept once again the fact there are people placed in powerful positions and have lost sight of right and wrong?

Breakstone felt teachers and staff need to better understand that every decision in the life of a child and teenager under their care can make a permanent impact. To leave a seat empty at graduation may help Gabe's f riends heal and find some closure. Or perhaps the empty seat would bring attention to teen suicide and perhaps more can be done to look for the signs and prevent this from happening.

Most of all, the empty seat would help Gabe's friends remember the good times they had with him.

Breakstone didn't want this turned into a controversy, but it seemed to him if the seat was left open, the school would honor Gabe as a student who loved the ocean and equally loved others.

Instead, the seat was taken away, which to Breakstone, felt like the school was remembering Gabe's final action in his life and the reason he wasn't here.

Why does it always seem the world has the final say, rather than God?

Breakstone needed to find the answer…

"Our teenagers have lost a lot of dear friends in the last twelve months. There is a lot of unity among the kids but a lot of quiet hurt. Let's all hug our young friends and family a little bit more. It's okay to talk about loss. Much better than silently hoping it goes away. I miss you Gabriel Breakstone and I love you." ~ Shalom Breakstone

115

When Breakstone walked along the beach on Siesta Key, his thoughts drifted to the night they lit a candle for Gabe and sent the lantern's into the night sky, floating over the Gulf of Mexico.

As for today, on Breakstone's walk in the white sand, it was during the day with a mixture of light rain and sun, but for some reason, the weather felt perfect.

Breakstone stopped and gazed to the far end of the water. Suddenly a rainbow appeared and took his breath away.

In the bible, the rainbow represents a promise from God. In this moment, God was telling Breakstone that the rainbow was completing Gabe's beautiful journey.

Breakstone dropped to his knees, tears flowing from his eyes, thanking God for all those who knew Gabe. He made people laugh, he made them cry, but most of all, Gabe had this power to make people feel something deep inside themselves.

Perhaps an empty seat in the high school wasn't important after all. Gabe had taken a seat in Heaven with the Lord Almighty.

What better place to sit than that?

"I have set the Lord always before me. Because He is at my right hand, I will not be shaken." ~ Psalm 16:8

116

Breakstone woke in the middle of the night, sitting straight up from bed. God had spoken to him.

Or was it just a dream?

No! It was more than a dream! God spoke directly to Breakstone's heart!

So many of his family and friends had gone through difficult times in their lives. In most cases, all of them felt alone, like in a desert. Loneliness turns into dry times, leaving people in a difficult place.

Breakstone's father used to always say to him, "Steve, desert soil is some of the most fertile soil around; it just needs water."

Breakstone craved to do a new thing. With God's help, new rivers and springs can be created in the wilderness and wastelands.

God will bring the living water into his life and to others. Breakstone had to let God use the example of his life to illustrate God's majesty and reveal the spring of life.

There are so many people Breakstone could reach. There was a reason God permitted so many things to slip away.

Breakstone's marriage.

His job.

Joe.

His reputation.

Worst of all…his son.

Being left at rock bottom in the middle of the desert, God could now use Breakstone for His good. God promised to love him and never leave Breakstone alone again.

There are so many possibilities for the future. Breakstone was anxious to move forward, using God's wisdom as the path to greatness.

"Watch for the new thing I am going to do. It is happening already…you can see it now! I will make a road through the wilderness and give you streams of water there." ~ Isaiah 43:19

117

Breakstone pondered in awe how he'd failed and dishonored Jesus so many times that he couldn't count. As for Jesus, He could count Breakstone's failures, but He chooses not to, because Christ loves in a way that Breakstone could not fully perceive.

Yet Breakstone realized how much work he needed to do because he craved the wisdom to not count all the times people have wronged him, but instead, find a way to fully love them no matter what, just as Christ had done.

In 1 Timothy 1:15-16, there's a trustworthy saying that deserves full acceptance: "Christ Jesus came into the world to save sinners, of whom I am the worst. But for that very reason I was shown mercy so that in me, the worst of sinners, Christ Jesus might display his immense patience as an example for those who would believe in him and receive eternal life."

118

Most everyone knows the verse Jeremiah 29:11, "For I know the plans I have for you declares the Lord, plans to prosper you and not to harm you, plans to give you hope and a future." However, Breakstone wanted to understand the words on a much deeper level.

Backing up to verse 10, Breakstone read, "This is what the Lord says: When seventy years are completed for Babylon, I will come to you and fulfill my gracious promise to bring you back to this place."

Then jumping to verses 12-14, "Then you will call upon me and come and pray to me, and I will listen to you. You will seek me with all your heart. I will be found by you declares the Lord, and will bring you back from captivity."

Breakstone thought about his "Babylon's" and his "Captivity."

His problems had been created by his own stiff neck, just like the Israelites. God only allowed Babylon and Captivity so that Breakstone would one day fall to his knees and seek God.

Now, he's more aware of what can block his eyes from seeing love, patience, kindness, wisdom, strength, and God's path for him.

Sharing this with others, just as Breakstone did with Joe, would be a calling that will last until his last breath.

"And we know that all things work together for good to those who love God, to those who are the called according to His purpose." ~ Romans 8:28

119

What happens when you find yourself in ruins? Breakstone prays that people will barely hear him, but yet will see God clearly.

There were times when Breakstone felt alone, but it wasn't true, especially when he committed to walk with God.

When Breakstone was four-years-old, his father abandoned the family and took off. Before he walked out the door, Breakstone told his father, "Dad, please don't go."

He left anyway.

Breakstone's mother never said the words, "I love you." It never really bothered him, except he carried this tradition on with his own family for a long time. Those simple three words could have made such a difference if he would found them earlier in his marriage and with his children.

When Breakstone was sixteen, his mother had become a fulltime alcoholic. There was an incident when Breakstone asked a girl to the prom. When he was going to leave, his mother asked, "Aren't you going to bring your date inside so I can see her?"

Breakstone shook his head and said, "No. I don't want you embarrassing me."

His mother reacted by biting him on the arm until she drew blood.

On many occasions, he would stand in front of the mirror, gaze into his own eyes and say with determination, "You're going to get out of here."

There was another incident when she became violently drunk. Breakstone was in his bedroom and his mother was down below in the living room with a gun. She raised the gun to the ceiling and fired. The bullet shot through the floor and just missed him.

Breakstone allowed the ruins of his parents to create ruins in himself.

Breakstone's older brothers and sisters had been given to separate foster homes by his mother and grandmother, which caused more emotional problems for Breakstone.

He questioned who would leave him next. Also, would anyone close to him be taken away?

It shouldn't have been an excuse to act the way he did, however, if Breakstone would have discovered the grace of God earlier in life and acted upon that grace, his life would have been completely different.

Instead, Breakstone used his army training and police training to control his emotions. He never read the bible or went to church. Things like that were for people who had weaknesses.

Breakstone had to prove that his parents weren't going to destroy him.

When it was all said and done, the only person who could destroy Breakstone was Breakstone.

"These things I have spoken to you, that in Me you may have peace. In the world you will have tribulation; but be of good cheer, I have overcome the world." ~ 1 Peter 5:6-7

120

Over time as Breakstone strengthened his faith, he began to love reading Proverbs each day. Solomon was considered one of the wisest and richest men of all times. In fact, he became sort of a mentor for Breakstone on how to mentor others, even with difficulties in his own life.

Breakstone read Proverbs 4:7 which said, "Getting wisdom is the most important thing you can do."

Then in Proverbs 4:23, "Above all else guard your heart for it is the wellspring of life." Another version says, "Be careful how you think; your life is shaped by your thoughts."

Solomon knew that wisdom was the most valuable treasure. He even asked for it over wealth and received both. But when he says to guard your heart for it is the wellspring of life, Breakstone believed Solomon revealed that heart knowledge is greater than head knowledge.

This means heart knowledge is the love of God, mercy, and grace. There are great things that people must understand and they are often the most profound to embrace.

Everything Breakstone went through with his divorce, the media bashing, the loss of his son, and the loss of Joe, in some profound way must be embraced. If Breakstone used his head as a basis of knowledge, then he for sure will end up in his old habits.

Instead, Breakstone had to guard his mind by using the wisdom God placed in his heart.

Breakstone could imagine Gabe and Joe meeting in heaven, giving each other a hand slap and hug, then talking about how fortunate they were to know Jesus while spending what little time they had on earth.

Gabe and Joe are both praying for all those young men and women who need to hear the Word of God.

It's not easy to think about how Gabe made the choice to kill himself. It was a choice made in his drifting thoughts, rather than listening to the wisdom in his heart.

Joe listened to his mind when deciding to become a leader in the street, rather than listening to his heart to become a leader of a church.

Their memory could be viewed as tragic, however, that's not how Breakstone remembered his son and Joe.

Breakstone remembered their love…this is what propels him forward.

"But when these things begin to take place, straighten up and lift up your heads, because your redemption is drawing near." ~ Luke 21:28

Dream It.

Believe It.

Pray for It.

Do what successful people do.

"According to your faith…let it be done to you." ~ Matthew 9:29

Steve Breakstone

Isaiah, Sonya, Shalom and Gabriel

Camp Choice PSI Ranch

ACKNOWLEDGMENTS

I would like to acknowledge all the people who have been examples of love in my life. Some of them continued to love me, even when I was acting in an unworthy manner. It would be impossible to name all of you. There isn't enough paper printed.

To my children Sonya, Isaiah, Gabriel, and Shalom, "I love you like there's no tomorrow." Thank you for helping me, even during the times when you helped in silence.

To my (step) dad Lester Breakstone who is in heaven. You taught me so much about being a man and how to find a way to get things done.

To the best mirror I ever met, Bobbi Hunt; you showed me what I didn't believe existed.

To PSI Seminars, Kathy Quinlan Perez and the whole PSI family. Thank you for helping me find freedom of spirit.

Lindford Sommers, John Malone, and so many more thank you for prayers, support, and being an example.

To Shirley McGriff, Joes mom, who is in heaven waiting on me with a big hug. You called me every day without fail for seventeen years and became my mom and the greatest example of love this side of Jesus.

To so many, many others…I love you all and THANK YOU FOR BELIEVING IN ME!

Steve Breakstone

Joe's Mom Shirley

CPSIA information can be obtained
at www.ICGtesting.com
Printed in the USA
LVHW080309030722
722649LV00032B/490